HANNAH, DIVIDED

Also by Adele Griffin

Amandine

Dive

The Other Shepards

Sons of Liberty

Split Just Right

Rainy Season

Witch Twins

Witch Twins at Camp Bliss

HANNAH, DIVIDED

ADELE GRIFFIN

HYPERION BOOKS FOR CHILDREN

NEW YORK

First Edition

1 3 5 7 9 10 8 6 4 2

Printed in the United States of America

Library of Congress Cataloging-in-Publication Data on file.

ISBN 0-7868-0879-9 (trade edition)

ISBN 0-7868-2664-9 (library edition)

Visit www.hyperionchildrensbooks.com

For my aunt, Elizabeth Sands

CONTENTS

PART THREE

PART ONE

1

THE CITY VISITOR

NEVER HAD Brintons Bridge School looked so presentable. Its floor had been swept, its windows and chalkboard washed, its standing globe dusted, and a jam jar of marigolds placed on the windowsill. Never had its students appeared so scrubbed, either. Miss Cascade had asked them to pay close attention to fingernails, necks, and ears. Even Elgin Winnicker's cowlick was spit-flattened neat to the back of his head.

All this fuss in preparation for Mr. Sweet, who, according to Miss Cascade, "just might be

3

the most influential gentleman, ever, to step through our door."

Hannah Bennett turned the words over in her head. *Most influential gentleman, ever.* She pictured Mr. Sweet as a combination of Moses and Charles Darwin. Only, Mr. Sweet was not traveling from Egypt or the Galápagos, but from Philadelphia, and he was coming to give their school money. Perhaps. Miss Cascade had read his letter out loud, the one he had written in response to Miss Cascade's request for aid from the Wexler Foundation, the charitable trust for which Mr. Sweet worked. Mr. Sweet's answer had been not quite yes but not quite no. *Perhaps,* he had written.

That was why their schoolhouse looked sharp as a needle today. To help push Mr. Sweet's answer away from *perhaps* and closer to *yes.*

Miss Cascade looked up from her desk to waggle a finger at her students. "Class, we must remember politeness," she said. "Everyone knows that our school needs a new roof and modern textbooks. Politeness counts." Her eyes darted to Hannah, who often forgot about politeness.

Hannah lifted her chin and straightened. She had been helping the fifth graders with their long-division problems. She had been good all day and would continue to be so. She would not vex and disappoint.

Peggy Stone pulled at Hannah's sleeve. "Hannah, my answer turned out to be not enough numbers."

"Because you forgot the decimal point, Peggy." Hannah picked up the pencil and dotted it in. "Five point one and point five one are different amounts when you—"

Her concentration broke with the faint sound of a car's engine, gurgling and chugging down Brintons Bridge Road. Was that a motorcar? But nobody arrived at school by car! She leaped out of her seat and ran to the window.

"He's here! It's Mr. Sweet from Philadelphia!"

"Hannah! Sit down!"

"Lookatit, lookit his automobile! Brand

spanking new! That's a swell lot of money, I'll say!"

Books banged to the floor as students jumped from benches to cram into the schoolhouse's open doorway. The polite, pent-up waiting of the afternoon was broken.

"A Super Eight Packard Touring," breathed Elgin, who was nuts for automobiles and could name every model. "Musta just rolled out of big Bay City!"

"Could be quite a chunk of money sunk in that Wexler fund, if Mr. Sweet can arrive in such style," said Betsy Seal.

"Girls, boys!" implored Miss Cascade. "Hannah!"

But once on her feet, Hannah could hardly bring herself to sit down again. The banana-yellow Packard veered off the road, stirring up a riot of dust, and charged the narrower graveled footpath to the school's front door, where it hiccuped to a stop. Its engine gurgled and cut, and the driver's-side door jerked open on oiled hinges. Hannah stared as one two-toned shoe, then another, planted itself to the ground. How peculiar—Mr. Sweet wore ladies' shoes! Then the rest of a strong, stout woman emerged.

"Miss Cascade?" The woman's voice was a bellow.

"Yes! Yes, I am! And you—?"

"Mrs. Theodora Ann Sweet!" the woman announced. "From the Wexler Foundation of Philadelphia! My friends call me Teddy. So may you!" She offered the favor grandly.

"*Mrs.!*—Teddy—Sweet!" Miss Cascade disguised her surprise with a friendly smile. "Please, madam, won't you come in? By your name, I mistakenly thought . . ."

Mrs. Sweet was not listening. She palmed shut the car door as if she were closing a vault. Then she used her handkerchief to spit and rub at a smudge on the side window. "Mitts off my baby!" she ordered as she faced them. "She's only three months old!"

Ignoring Miss Cascade's offered hand, she

barreled up the short flight of stone steps to the schoolhouse. Students parted at the door to give her way. A fearsome woman, Hannah thought, but so smartly dressed, in a gray suit cut thick as a slipcover, and matching tipped beret over her dark, bronze-rinsed hair. A silk sprig of lilac drooped sideways from her lapel, and an envelope bag fell slantwise from one broad shoulder.

Hannah counted seven suit buttons, eleven footsteps, and five syllables in her name. From bag to beret, Theodora Sweet seemed to be an odd-numbered, slant-sided sort of person.

Miss Cascade shooed boys and girls back to their seats while Mrs. Sweet's gaze skipped across the room for a chair. Finding none, she scooted herself up onto the dunce stool, which caused a surge of giggling. Miss Cascade frowned the room into quiet.

Unconcerned, Mrs. Sweet pulled a clipboard and pen from her envelope bag. "Even for backwoods Chadds Ford farmland, this school is teensy-weensy! How many are you?"

"I teach fifty-six students." Miss Cascade stood in front of her desk, her politeness smile now stretched into place. "Some of our older boys have left to work their family farms for the harvest. We'll get them in school again before the first frost."

"What bad form, to interrupt schooling with farming." Mrs. Sweet scribbled on her clipboard. Left-handed, with her legs crossed and head inclined, she looked slightly skewed. Hannah tilted her own head to observe the woman better. "Let's see." Mrs. Sweet used her pen as a pointer. "Stove in back, organ in front. . . . Is that the door to the W.C.?"

"To the cellar, where we store wood and coal," answered Miss Cascade. "We have a separate facility out back for our . . . ablutions."

"Well, hold my hat! An outdoor can, in this day and age!" Mrs. Sweet spoke in such a boom that another wave of laughter swept the schoolhouse and again was calmed by Miss Cascade's strict eye.

Hannah peered down her row at the line of folded hands and upturned faces, each boy and girl hoping to win Miss Cascade's approval and Mrs. Sweet's charity. Didn't anyone care that Mrs. Sweet was rude and bossy? Calling their school "backwoods" and "teensy-weensy"! Making fun of their outhouse!

"Give us our money, and good riddance," Hannah murmured.

Betsy turned and pushed a finger to her lips. "Hannah, gracious! Hush!"

"Each row is grade-divided. First to eighth. After graduating, most will continue on to the Consolidated School." Miss Cascade's smile now seemed pulled against its will. "Here, the older ones tutor the younger. We enjoy reading and ciphering and history and music. We put on a pageant every spring. All of my students partic-ipate, and we invite most everyone in Chester County to come see it."

"Lovely." Mrs. Sweet made no attempt to hide her yawn. But Miss Cascade's pageants were wonderful! Certainly nothing to yawn about! Was nobody going to speak up for them?

"Miss Cascade! Tell how last spring, we did a tribute to Benjamin Franklin!" Hannah called out on impulse. "Tell how my big brother Roy was Mr. Franklin himself, and he was so good! How he wore a pigtail and flew a kite and signed the Declaration of—"

"Hannah!" Miss Cascade interrupted. "What do I say about talking out of turn?"

"Oh, pageants are fine sport." Mrs. Sweet flicked her fingers. "But they're no education. Nor is having older children teach the babies." Her eyebrow lifted. "Isn't that so?"

Nobody answered. Nobody laughed, either. Mrs. Sweet's words were mean. They sliced open the school and dismissed it as if it were bruised fruit. Hannah bit her lips to stop from shouting that she *loved* teaching math to the younger students. In fact, math was the only subject where she felt clever. Enough with this visitor, this snooty Mrs. Sweet! They didn't need her goodwill. Their old school roof would do—it only leaked in back, and Miss Cascade caught the water easily enough using bread pans.

Hannah looked to her teacher to see what she might say next. Miss Cascade smoothed her white bib. Hot spots of color had appeared on her cheeks.

"These are the times we're living in, er, Teddy," explained Miss Cascade. "In our schoolhouse, the most important lesson we learn is to help one another. It's true there isn't much extra to go around. But nothing gets wasted, either."

Mrs. Sweet waved off Miss Cascade's words. "And nothing gets accomplished!"

The shifts and whispers among the others agreed that now Mrs. Sweet didn't seem half as nice as her name or her car. She was far from Hannah's image of "the most influential gentleman, ever."

"What a snob," Hannah murmured. "That's the last time I pick marigolds for Mrs. *Sour.*"

This time, nobody shushed her.

"HARK! AH, THE NIGHTINGALE—"

WHEN MISS CASCADE dismissed the class for the day, her finger pinned Hannah back to her seat.

"Hannah," she said. "Don't go yet. I want Mrs. Sweet to have a word with you."

Boys and girls were bouncing toward the door.

"Mitts off my baby!" warned Mrs. Sweet.

Betsy and Tru looked at Hannah pityingly as they collected their lunch pails and stuffed their books into their satchels.

"Remember, be *polite*, Hannah," said Frank Dilworth. "It'd be nice to have new books and such."

"But don't let that city slicker bother you about your reading," whispered Betsy.

"I will. I won't. See you tomorrow." Hannah could feel her face reddening under the sympathetic eyes of the departing students. Everyone knew why Hannah was being kept inside.

Boys and girls jostled out the door as Hannah dragged herself to the first-row bench at the front of the room. Miss Cascade waved good-bye and called last-minute reminders. Mrs. Sweet stood by the window and kept an eye on her Packard. Now it was only the three of them as the others swarmed, free as bees, down the road.

"Mrs. Sweet, this is Hannah Bennett," said Miss Cascade, perching next to Hannah. "I had mentioned her in my letter to you."

She had? How shameful! Hannah set her chin and stared unblinking at the chalkboard.

"Yes. The illiterate." Mrs. Sweet dropped

heavily on the bench at Hannah's other side. Her voice, loud and tired, was like that of a deaf doctor who has made too many house calls in one day.

Hannah's eyes did not move from the board. It's not so awful that I can't read, she thought miserably, as it is to be singled out and scolded for it. Though Miss Cascade's voice was gentle as she spoke. "During my three years here, I have done everything in my power to teach Hannah to read. Sadly, I haven't made progress. Hannah cannot see the structure of a sentence. She confuses word order. Is this something you've come across in your visits to other schools?"

"Certainly!" Mrs. Sweet snapped. "And I'd bet that sloth is at the root of it. Sloth is our undoing!"

Already she was rummaging through Hannah's book sack. She tugged from it Hannah's most dreaded schoolbook, *My Poem and Verse Companion*, and flipped its soft pages.

"Ah, 'Philomela'! Miss Bennett, what do you see when you look at 'Philomela'?" She held the open book aloft, cracking its spine.

Hannah stared. "Letters."

"Don't be fresh about Matthew Arnold, miss! We *all* see letters! When arranged into groups, they are called words!"

"I didn't mean—I meant . . ." Hannah took a breath. Politeness first, she reminded herself. She would not disappoint Frank and Betsy and the others. "The letters make a pattern. The *t*s and the *l*s and the *r*s." She leaned forward to examine them.

"These words are simple and lovely," needled Mrs. Sweet. "Read them, don't fear them!"

Fear them? Was Mrs. Sweet trying to provoke her? Hannah stared, hard-eyed, at the words, each packed in like a boxcar of letters, willing her to unload it, to count and stack its contents into a proper grouping.

She tapped the page corners with her finger and stared across the first line.

H a r k ! a h , t h e n i g h t i n g a l e—

Hark!ahthenightingale

Hhh aaa r k tt ee nn ii gg l

16

"Three *h*s, three *a*s, r, k, double *t*, two *e*s, two *n*s, two *i*s, double *g*, *l*," she said. She scanned down the page, collecting *e*s. "The *e*s will likely win in the end."

Miss Cascade made a clucking sound. "Hannah is quite good in math," she asserted. "Multiplication tables and fractions and her long division."

"Well, that's nothing to sneeze at," said Mrs. Sweet. "What's nine times seven?"

"Nine times seven," Hannah repeated. By now, though, 'Philomela' had spiraled itself like a kaleidoscope into her eye, burying the answer to nine times seven beneath it. She filled the air with a whisper of other numbers: "One point two eight five seven—" before it washed to surface. "Sixty-three!" She pressed a hand to her heart. "How could I forget? Sixty-three!"

"Hannah, softer, please," whispered Miss Cascade. "We're right here."

"I do know my times tables, truly," Hannah assured Mrs. Sweet. "And my ma said that if I was no better at reading this year, she'd teach me next summer. We'll use the Bible. The Bible ought to have every word I'd ever use! So don't trouble yourself over me, ma'am."

She was not speaking politely enough. Mrs. Sweet looked from Hannah to Miss Cascade to Hannah again.

"One point two eight . . . " she murmured. "And how many ts in 'Philomela'?"

Hannah glanced at the page and the number flew across her mind like a blackbird. "Seventy-four."

"Hannah, dear," reproved Miss Cascade. "Don't answer as if you *know*."

"Hmm." Mrs. Sweet flipped the page. "Oh, gorgeous! William Wordsworth, 'Strange Fits of Passion Have I Known.' Count the *a*s, please?"

In the pause of the next moment, Hannah sensed a crackle of attention on either side of her. Ma had long warned her not to show off her counting trick. It was peculiar, Ma said, and put people on edge, like speaking backward.

Counting off numbers—if it must be done—ought to be similar to reciting bedtime prayers. A private comfort, said Ma, though Granddad McNaughton saw it differently. Proud of her math, he liked Hannah to show it off a bit.

"The *as*," Mrs. Sweet repeated. So vexing! Egging Hannah on.

And the answer was irresistible. "Forty-three."

Miss Cascade laughed. "Oh, that couldn't . . . it's not true." She snatched the book from Mrs. Sweet. Her lips moved silently as her finger popped along the page. "Forty-two. A very good guess, though, Hannah."

"You missed one," Hannah said. "Your finger skipped the second *a* in *wayward*."

Mrs. Sweet snatched the book and cut to another place. "Aha. Christina Rossetti, 'The Goblin Market.' Four pages! Count the *p*s. All of them!" Her tone dared Hannah to try.

Hannah took the book onto her lap. The pattern was beautiful, big and small *p*s flicking their tails like fish. Her mind dropped over them like a net, caught and counted them into their proper school. "Two hundred twenty-eight."

"The *r*s!"

The small *r*s were curved canes; their upper cases walked on two legs under fat stomachs. "Nine hundred thirty-one."

"And the *e*s?"

Ah, wonderful *e*s, the lower *e*s in clusters like tiny mushrooms to be picked, with a single uppercase *E* standing alone as a broken ladder. Hannah gathered them all up. "One thousand, seven hundred eleven."

Mrs. Sweet's snort startled Hannah from her counting trance. "Now, this is poetry, Miss Cascade!" she cried. "Strange poetry, but nonetheless! The girl can read numbers into eternity! How could you not have known?" She laughed in a pleased but startled way.

Miss Cascade was not laughing. "Goodness, Hannah, you never made use of this . . . *game* during math class." She shut the book and held it on her lap as if it were Pandora's box. She seemed stumped as to what to say next.

"I don't take math, Miss Cascade," Hannah reminded. "I tutor it. You told me in the beginning of last year that I'd learned all the math skills I'd ever need. You wanted me to concentrate on my reading." *And that math was more practical for boys.* Hannah kept that part to herself, as well as the fact that Granddad McNaughton had been tutoring her privately for years. Poor Miss Cascade looked upset enough.

"Miss Cascade is correct. Reading *is* essential, for a full and productive life." Mrs. Sweet peered at Hannah with something like hunger in her eyes. It made Hannah feel uncomfortable, but a tiny thrill of pride swelled through her, too. If nothing else, she had impressed both Mrs. Sweet and Miss Cascade with her counting.

She returned Mrs. Sweet's gaze directly. "I don't much care about being illiterate, Mrs. Sweet, especially when there's so many others—my best friends, Tru and Betsy, plus Ma and my brother Roy—to read aloud to me. Ma says there's bigger problems in our country than not understanding when the *e* is silent." She drew a breath. "And if you must know, I don't care for poetry, either. Thankfully, it's our first class, so I don't have to dread—"

"All right, Hannah." Miss Cascade lifted and dropped her hands. "I think we're finished here. Get along home. Your family will be wondering."

Mrs. Sweet nodded in agreement. Hannah leaped from her seat and nearly knocked over the dunce stool on her way out the door.

"Take heed, Hannah," warned Miss Cascade. To Mrs. Sweet, she said, "You must understand, her difficulties are greater than you perceive. I can't see how you might think . . ."

Hannah was not listening. She did not much care what Mrs. Sweet might think. She ducked outside, floating into the warm welcome of a September afternoon. Free.

3

RUNNING, COUNTING, STACKING

HANNAH DECIDED to run home.

She had to. The counting had given her energy. It was like performing a circus entertainment, like spinning plates or eating fire. Counting was a bolt of hot, bright lightning in her brain. It was a habit and a comfort, yes, but it also opened her mind to a vastness of numbers that overwhelmed her.

No matter how fast Hannah ran, she could always count faster.

She was counting, even now. She had started with the poems and she could not stop.

She counted her steps, the draw and release of her breath. She counted fence posts, birds, Holsteins, rocks strewn along her path.

She counted inside things, too. Rounded up this afternoon to four o' clock and from there, she counted off the hours until the dawn of her birthday, April fourteenth. Then she counted the hours she had lived since her last taste of chocolate ice cream, the minutes her seventy-nine-year-old self would be on this earth at eight in the morning of the first day of the year 2001 (factoring in the 1,440 minutes per extra day times 20 leap years).

Finally, she took this year, 1934, and divided it by two. Over and over, skipping the decimal point like a checkers piece until it stood at the front of the line.

Granddad McNaughton encouraged her mathematics. Sunday afternoons, they passed gleeful hours inventing games with figures and sums, making up riddles and puzzles to solve. Until recently, Granddad himself was always up and running, too, either to clear branches or chop wood or weed his vegetable garden. Mental tasks must be balanced by the physical, Granddad liked to say. He'd been feeling poorly of late, but he never said no to a walk in the outdoors. And he still loved math.

Hannah's shoes were thick with dust by the time she turned off Brintons Bridge Road and onto Orchard Way. The same sprint, an equal length of distance, every step. She rounded the Applebee farm and the Roe farm and Indian Rock. Objects whizzed by, and she gathered them mentally, easy as *p*s and *r*s and *t*s.

It was not until she reached her front gate that she stopped and stood, panting, triumphant. She closed her eyes to set the final sums in a row.

Steps: 1, 657

Paired breaths: 520

Fence posts: 192

Birds: 29

Holsteins: 44

Rocks: 170 (gray: 111; black: 53; mixed: 6)

Hours left until April 14: 5,041

Hours since last taste of chocolate ice cream: 3,212

Minutes lived on planet Earth at eight o'clock A.M. of 1/1/2001: 41,927,680

1934 divided: 967, 483.5, 241.75, 120.875, 60.4375, 30.1875, 15.09375, 7.546875, 3.7734375, 1.8867188, .9433594

4

LATE

MA WAS TAKING down the bedsheets in the side yard and listening to the kitchen radio tuned to *The Betty Crocker Hour*. Hannah saw her undergarments flapping on the line. Not again—as if she hadn't asked Ma a thousand times to please let her dry her delicates in the privacy of her bedroom!

But Ma, always busy and never modest about such things, often forgot.

Hannah dashed across the yard, shouting a flapping, strutting Homer out of her way, then

jumped for a pair of waving underpants. She jig-
gled the line hard. Roy's spare coveralls and one
of Pa's kerchiefs dropped to the dirt.

"Careful, Hannah! Look before you leap."

Hannah had heard that warning too many
times to pay attention to it. She yanked down an
undershirt and folded it over her arm. "Ma, I've
wished a hundred times you would allow me care
of my own underclothes."

"If wishes were horses . . ." Ma answered.
"Hurry now. You're late to milking."

"Ladies, you may also use honey or Karo
syrup in place of white sugar," assured the gentleman announcer.

Ha! Karo syrup was a special-occasions treat.
In fact, most sweet food was a special-occasions
treat. The announcer ought to stick to explaining
Bisquick and red cabbage. But *The Betty Crocker
Hour* was Ma's favorite show, and Hannah knew
better than to talk over it.

She hurried into the house and upstairs to her
bedroom. Her underwear was dried stiff enough

to put away. She took care to fold each article just so before placing it in her clothes cupboard, though Ma wearied of Hannah's insistence on ruler-straight edges and right angles, on stacking every pair of stockings and underwear neat as saucers.

"Your habits have more hold on you than you do on them," Ma often chided.

Hannah shut the cupboard and stood at the window an extra moment, feeling the house all around her as she looked out over the view. She stared across the field to the barn's red roof, half-hidden in a green canopy of maples. Here in her bedroom, across the hall from the room where she'd been born, and staring out over the low hills at a spread of family-owned property—here was safety. She tapped a pattern on the paint-thickened windowpane. She loved her home, with its swept corners and known secrets, its worn, dark furniture, its every scent and view familiar to her.

And now it was September. Soon the leaves

would change color, and there would be much to reap for the autumn harvest. In addition to the dairy, the farm had a small oat piece, a potato piece, a garden piece, as well as three acres of orchard. Come winter, sacks of feed would be put away for the livestock, as well as potatoes stacked next to cans of pickled cucumbers, stewed tomatoes, and jar upon jar of Hannah's favorite preserves, plum and peach, which she and Ma likely would be pitting until late October.

Late! Quickly, Hannah shed her school clothes for milking slacks and a sweater. Then she tied on her white floursack apron, knotting it twice around her middle. The apron was an old one of Ma's, and though Hannah was taller, she didn't have quite Ma's girth yet.

On the way out to the barn, she checked her reflection in the tarnished kitchen mirror. It stopped her. She batted her eyes and gave her best movie-star smile. Then she peered harder at herself. Her face, swamped in a quantity of pale, flyaway hair, looked soft and indistinct. She wished she were a more precise-looking person, with Joan Crawford's hurt, liquid eyes or with the sly smirk of Claudette Colbert. But the face in the mirror might belong to any girl.

"Hannah!" Her mother's voice broke Hannah from her thoughts. She turned. Ma stood in the doorway, the laundry basket at her hip, Hannah's milk buckets held out in her opposite hand. "There's a sight. Gazing at yourself when you're needed in the milk house. Where is your sense?"

"I'm going, I'm going." Hannah collected the buckets and ducked out the door.

Down at the milk house, Roy, Pa, and Ben were finishing up. The cows were back in the barn, fed and content, and Ben was washing down the floor to its center drain. When he saw Hannah, he nodded acknowledgment and looked away.

The year before, when Ben had come to work for the family, Hannah had decided he was a terrible grouch. Now she knew better: that Ben was a private man, given to long fits of low spirits, pining for his wife and son in Ohio. He almost never spoke of them, but he sent his pay home every month, riding with Pa in the pickup into town and handing the envelope to the postmaster as if it contained a living thing.

Pa said that Ben was lucky to have work when most men didn't, though *lucky* was not the word that came to Hannah's mind. *Lonely* fit Ben better.

Roy and Pa were huddled in the corner, gingerly lowering the last milk cans into the new electric cooler. They'd only had it for two months, every spare nickel of last year and most of this one sunk into its purchase. But the dairy had been bedeviled by the need for the cooler (Pa's words), and since the farm almost never earned out in plain cash money, the cooler had been a long time in the waiting. It was here now, and better than any Christmas gift, Hannah reasoned, as this winter she and Roy would not have to pry up ice from the pond to keep the milk chilled overnight.

"Hannah, where've you been to?" asked Pa. "We could have used your touch roundabout a half hour ago. Dosey was acting persnickety."

"I was held back after school. They had a special lady come in from some charity in Philadelphia. I suppose Miss Cascade thought she'd have the right answer to my reading problem."

"And did she?" Pa took off his cap and wiped his forehead with it. He looked upset. School and reading had been a struggle for him, as well. "Think she might tighten some screws in your noggin?"

"They'll tighten themselves, Pa," Hannah assured him. She refrained from saying more. Pa would not want to hear about the other part of the visit, about her counting letters and the surprise that washed over Mrs. Sweet's and Miss Cascade's faces. No, that was a show-off story; a tale for Granddad's ears alone.

"C'mon, cover these, lollygagger!" called Roy. He disliked it when he had to pull Hannah's share.

She got to work. All that was left to do was to fasten the straining cloths over the two remaining milk cans and to secure the fabric in place with wooden clothespins, a final step before the cans were stored in the cooler until tomorrow morning's delivery.

She was good at fastening. The cloth spread evenly, no puckering, smooth as a painter's canvas.

"Radio ought to wipe out most recreational reading altogether," said Pa after a few moments, speaking to Hannah in a burst as if he'd been stewing on it. "Folks hear faster than they can read, and it's no strain to the eyes neither."

Hannah nodded. She liked that idea.

EVENING SURPRISE

HEPP'S LETTER, unopened in the middle of the table, would be more sumptuous than dessert. Ma planned to read it out loud after dinner. Roy, who could mow through a plate of food in two minutes, kicked Hannah under the table to hurry her. She paid no mind and ate her usual way—clockwise, after arranging the food around her plate from least to greatest. Biscuit, rice, bacon lardons, sliced tomato.

Pa stirred all the food on his plate into a puddle and sank a pool of gravy in the middle, as did Ben, but a look from Ma made Roy decide against it. Ma didn't hold Hannah and Roy to much proper behavior, but she'd been a doctor's daughter before she became a farmer, and she kept an entire set of rules like a chest of antique silver tucked in a corner of her head.

As he did every night directly after supper, Ben stood and nodded his good-night, taking leave to smoke his pipe under the stars. Once Hannah had cleared the table and soaked the dishes, Ma reached for the letter.

"Shall we?"

"Yes!" chorused Hannah and Roy, while Pa stayed silent but took out his pipe.

Ma tickled her finger beneath the envelope flap, unable to wait another minute. It had been two years since Hepp left home, and everyone missed him sorely. Hepp was a full-grown twenty years old now and still footloose, "crisscrossing the states like a common tramp," in Pa's words.

Hepp's had not been a peaceful departure, either. Hannah could still recall the shouting in the living room, Hepp insisting that he'd never been a farmer and never would be one, and so he might as well take a look at the world and find the right spot to plant roots. Hepp was no good with the dairy, and he had as much feel for the land as the man in the moon. No, her oldest brother preferred wandering to any other activity, and he had spent most waking hours with his head lost in a book of travel or adventure.

But it was not until he'd left home that Hannah fully understood. Hepp out in the world also meant her world without Hepp. It grieved her. She kept one of his impossibly long socks in her dresser, along with the thick pamphlet Hepp had sent her from last year's World's Fair in Chicago. Only nothing was as nice as the sound of his voice, blending through Ma's as she read out loud.

Dear Family,

Except for the red chili peppers growing plentiful as crab apples, Santa Fe was a dead bust. Two weeks of picking and then

*no work, and now I'm twiddling my thumbs
in Macon. We'd had word there was hiring
out for cotton crops, seems we were wrong
and there's a hundred men for every job—
the usual story.*

*I got here by rail with my usual boys—
Fat Mike and Billy, and it took us three
days. We traded turns sleeping to keep an
eye skinned against the law. Okie Slims
and Texas Slims are quick to shoot you off
a train—only to scare, Ma, not to harm.
You'd laugh to see me, I swapped most of
what was in my bindle for food during a
stopover in Austin, so I use one map spread
over me for a blanket and the other folded
up for a pillow. We're hungry some, and
disappointed, but Mike's got a hunch to
head for Alabama. We hear there's pine
mills might need men for sawing—*

Ma broke off, startled at the noise. Pa
stopped knocking his pipe against the wall.

Hannah recognized the sound of that automobile. Mrs. Sweet! What was she doing here? Whether to discuss Hannah's poor reading or show-off counting, this unexpected visit would not likely please either Ma or Pa. Apprehension bunched in Hannah's chest as Roy leaped down the hall to throw open the door. There was a dog's belief in Roy that his brother might be coming home any day now.

Ma and Pa both scraped back their chairs and stood as Mrs. Sweet entered the kitchen in a bustle, introducing herself and pumping hands mightily all around.

"I'll sit, but I can't stay long!" she began when Pa indicated the vacant chair. "I have come to offer Hannah a once-in-a-lifetime opportunity, made possible by Wexler's generous auspices!"

"Wexler? I never heard of any Mister Wexler," said Pa, reseating himself when Mrs. Sweet settled into her chair. "He's not from these parts, anyhow."

"Because Wexler is a place, Pa, not a body,"

said Ma, moving to the kettle to prepare Mrs. Sweet a mug of hot tea.

"No, it's a thing," said Roy. "It's money, I bet."

For once, Hannah stayed as mute as if she'd been set on the dunce stool.

"It's a person, place, and thing!" Mrs. Sweet harrumphed. "It's a charitable trust, and I am its executive director, appointed by Philadelphia's own Mayor Moore. Part of our good work is to award scholarships to children who otherwise might not be receiving the usual advantages. So that he—or she—can prepare for a university education." She nodded thanks as she accepted the mug. "I did not travel out to these parts looking for a diamond in the rough, but it seems Hannah has a gift for numbers."

A gift for numbers. Hannah liked that, even if praise came from such a bossy-boots as Mrs. Sweet. And a scholarship! Well, wouldn't Granddad McNaughton be pleased to hear that!

Though one glance at her parents showed that they were not. "Oh, Hannah's got a *knack*," agreed Pa warily. "She does all the family invoicing. Puts the bills in the bottles at the end of the month. She's kept track of every cent for years. Course, farms don't get paid out always in money, so precision's not the upmost."

"Rest assured, Hannah would be taught more than invoicing!" retorted Mrs. Sweet. "She would be taught advanced concepts, algebra, geometry, proofs, theorems—"

"Madam, I ought to tell you now, it's a mighty far-fetched conversation we're having here," interrupted Ma. "It's not as if we have the money to send Hannah to a fancy university once you've taken all the effort to prepare her! And, it's not as if Hannah could qualify to study other subjects, what with all her reading troubles."

Pa nodded. He picked up Hepp's letter and began to fold it into small and smaller squares. Hannah knew that if Pa started to fold, things were knotting up inside his mind. "My wife speaks for us both," he said. "It's Hannah's reading where we'd like to see improvements. And truth be told," Pa added, "I don't myself see much point to girls learning fancy math."

"At Ottley Friends, in Philadelphia, Hannah will be reading quicker than you can say boo," said Mrs. Sweet. "As for girls and math, why, Mr. Bennett, we have lived to see Marie Curie twice win the Nobel Prize, once for Physics and once for Chemistry. Lord rest her soul."

Pa shook his head. "Cities are no use to children. Young ones are wild cockalorum and grown best out of doors." He set down Hepp's letter. His fidgeting fingers found and drew a long match from his breast pocket to strike against the table leg, and he turned his head from Mrs. Sweet to relight his pipe with slow, labored puffs.

"When did Miss Curie pass on?" asked Roy.

"This summer," answered Hannah. "And she was a doctor, not a miss, and it's pronounced cure-eee, not curry, dummy."

"Who's a dummy? It's not like *you* could've *read* it in the newspaper!" Roy scoffed.

"*Children,*" Ma scolded.

Mrs. Sweet turned to Hannah. "This is a wonderful chance, dear. Toward the end of December, state qualification exams are given to determine scholarship candidates. While Hannah prepares for them, she could lodge for the semester with me—or another sponsor family, if she prefers." Her voice began to frog into speechmaking tones as she addressed the room in general. "As a patron of Mayor Moore's education reform movement, I am an advocate of progress and learning experiments."

Hannah flinched. *Experiment* was the wrong word to use. The last experiment of Pa's had been to trade his best Holstein, Ruby, for two scrawny, deer-faced Jerseys, though Ruby gave more milk than the pair of them, and had a better temper besides. The last experiment of Ma's had been to repair the worn places in the kitchen tablecloth by patching it over in a cartwheel quilt pattern, but she hadn't had enough lemon-checked gingham to complete the design, and the tea-dyed woolsy she'd finished with gave the cloth a stained appearance.

"Roy, Hannah, go to your rooms," said Ma. "We'll move to the front room. This is grown-up talk now."

"I was going anyhow," said Roy in a low monotone as they both stood and shuffled from the kitchen. "Most boring conversation of my life."

Yet he looked upset, and he pushed past Hannah when he overtook her on the second-floor landing. "If you get to see the Liberty Bell before me, you're toasted and roasted," he said. "It's not fair, I'm almost fifteen, I read great—I was even Benjamin Franklin!—and I never saw Philadelphia. Not one blamed time. All I saw is New York City the way it looked in *King Kong*, which hardly counts a bean."

He slammed himself into his room, opened his door, and slammed it again.

There was no reasoning with Roy when he flared up that way.

Hannah crept to her own bedroom and looked out her window into the night. Treetops floated in a bath of fog, but the sky above was star-studded and clear. She breathed on the glass and drew circles with her finger. She spun her favorite number, thirty-two, through its cat's cradle of tricks. Thirty-two, the fifth power of two. Thirty-two pieces stood on a chessboard, and thirty-two were the numbers of teeth in a mouth—if none had been pulled.

Thirty-two would not stop Hannah's heart from pounding, though. She had to know what was being said below. At the very least, she should be allowed to hear enough to form her own opinion! She was owed that much, wasn't she?

After a few more minutes, she could not bear the suspense. On silent feet, she tiptoed back down the stairs. Mrs. Sweet was voicing her good-byes in the front hall. Too late! Before she could quite think it through, Hannah slipped around the corner, through the pantry, and out the kitchen door.

Mrs. Sweet had already swung through the gate to her Packard, which was parked at the edge of the lawn, looking as out of place as a sleeping yellow lion.

"Mrs. Sweet, ma'am?"

Mrs. Sweet turned. Hannah dropped to a walk, then stopped and held her ground, shifting her weight as she scratched a nagging itch of spider bite on her elbow. Now that she had Mrs. Sweet's attention, she was not sure what she wanted to say.

"Ah, Hannah." Mrs. Sweet shook her head. "Seems your parents are more country hardheads than I'd have figured. I'm sorry to fail you, but I'd easier talk a pair of parrots into reason."

Hannah frowned but stepped closer, resting each hand on a round-end picket post. "They're not hardheads, they're cautious, is all. And Ma's always said that counting numbers is no more than an odd trick."

"But you can do better than count, can't you, Hannah?" Mrs. Sweet leaned over the gate to speak in a hushed voice. She smelled like Pepsodent and sweet lilacs, as well as the more costly things of a world Hannah could not place.

"Nine times seven," prompted Mrs. Sweet. "I'm no fool! When I asked you what nine times seven was this afternoon, you divided it first, didn't you? Nine divided by seven is . . ."

Divided it? Hannah had not realized. "One point two . . . eight five seven one . . . one four—"

"That's not counting, see," interrupted Mrs. Sweet. "That's *calculating*."

"Calculating," Hannah echoed. It seemed too strong a word for what she'd done, slipping seven through the sieve of nine and sifting out the leftovers. "My granddad McNaughton . . ." she began, but her voice lost its way. *Speak up!* she commanded herself silently. She cleared her throat. "I was curious, ma'am. What's to d-do in Philadelphia?" she stammered.

"What's to do?" Mrs. Sweet looked

indignant. "Why, everything's to do! On a given Saturday, ladies and gentlemen attend the matinee and then stroll to the Bellevue-Stratford hotel for tea. There are ice sculptures and fountains there, and a woman in the tearoom who plays the harp like an angel. You can't find that here, can you?"

"My granddad McNaughton . . ." Hannah coughed again. She was floundering and she could see that Mrs. Sweet was losing patience with her. "Has been to Philadelphia," she finished.

"Lovely. And perhaps you'll see it one day, too. Or perhaps not. Look me up if you do," said Mrs. Sweet. Her voice was quick, false, done with talking. "*Au revoir*, Hannah. You're too young and ignorant to know the shame of this chance slipping you by, but remember one thing. It was Theodora Sweet who first spoke up for your math."

"That's not true!" Hannah exclaimed. "My granddad McNaughton has been speaking up for my math since I was little! He even sent away for a pamphlet about a special math school up in Boston, Massachusetts. He was thinking to take me to visit it this summer, but he hasn't been feeling himself lately. But it's Granddad who has the last word, see. Our farm is part McNaughton property." She stopped, horrified at what she had let slip out of her mouth. She clamped her hands together to stop from scratching her spider bite raw.

Silence held the air for a long moment before Mrs. Sweet spoke again. "Is that so?" she asked, her voice turned to honey, a coppery hook of eyebrow lifted. "Would it be helpful, then, Hannah, if I paid your grandfather a visit? McNaughton, is that his name?"

"Yes, ma'am." Hannah was glad the dark hid the flush in her face. Oh, she was in for it! Ma and Pa would fume with her for telling! But what was she supposed to do? She stepped back. "See him if you like, he lives just up the road—good night!"

"And good night to you, Hannah," said Mrs. Sweet as she wrenched open the car door. "Perhaps not all is lost."

Hannah allowed herself to scratch as soon as Mrs. Sweet ducked into her car and bumped down the road. Watched and scratched, until there was nothing to see but the smear of headlights aimed at the night ahead. The weight in her chest had become difficult to breathe through.

She consoled herself knowing that Granddad would have been furious with her if she hadn't spoken up. No gossip ever escaped Granddad's ears, and eventually he would have learned all about Mrs. Sweet. Hannah had grown used to the narrow seesaw she walked between pleasing Granddad and pleasing Ma and Pa. To suit her folks always meant putting Granddad's nose out of joint, and vice versa.

"I had to do it," Hannah said out loud, to reassure herself that it was so.

COFFEE OR TOBACCO

THE NEXT MORNING, Hannah woke earlier than usual. She bathed and dressed in her milking clothes—sweater, slacks, apron, boots—then crept downstairs to the kitchen to throw a pinecone and a few sticks of dry birch in the stove's hungry underbelly, stirring up the embers for breakfast.

Outdoors was chilly, the darkness like cool black silk thrown over the morning. She lit the gooseneck and collected her pail, placing both lamp and pail in the wheelbarrow, along with a first haul of glass bottles Ma had sterilized the afternoon before. The others would bring the rest. As she set off for the barn, lamplight cut out her shadow as it glided on the ground.

Ben, up and about first no matter how early anyone else rose, already had led a group of cows to the milk house, where Mouser was mewing for a first taste of the day. Hannah pulled up her stool in front of Dosey, then squirted the cat's face to appease and shoo him. Ben sat opposite.

"Bags washed, or do I need to?" she asked.

"Done," Ben replied.

Hannah made a loose loop in Dosey's tail and hung it on a tack so she wouldn't twitch—tail-twitching was Dosey's specialty—then got to work. The sound of milk, its swish and beat sure as a drum, was a morning rhythm as familiar as the hot breakfast that would follow. Mouser watched from the windowsill, licking his paws.

Soon, Pa and Roy stomped in. Roy began to lead the milked cows back to the barn and to collect another lowing, udder-heavy group to be relieved. Pa milked the Jerseys himself. Hannah knew her father well enough to hear impatience in the puff of his breath. He was still regretful about trading good old Ruby. But *No talking* was an unspoken rule of morning chores. Better to get the jobs finished and everyone's stomach filled—both animal and human—as soon as possible.

After the milking, Ben washed down the floor while Pa fed the cows. Roy and Hannah took care of the new supply; Roy pouring the translucent milk from the large cans into delivery quarts, which Hannah then fastened with cardboard lids and collars and hoisted into the wheelbarrow for Pa to cart to the truck. The air was cold enough that the cream was already separating to the top. On a winter morning, the milk would push the cream up over the cardboard, but temperatures would not drop to frost for another month at least.

"Your ma and I was up late," Pa said, slowing his gait to let Ben and Roy step ahead a pace as they all walked up to the house. "Talked about you, some."

"Me and Philadelphia?"

Pa's chin cut a quick yes and he cleared his throat. "We're set against it, Hannah. You've always been clever with your sums, nobody's arguing it, but there's too many cautions for us to rest easy. You've never traveled off the farm alone, and you're too young to be planked down in the middle of a big city. Neither your ma nor me reckon on Mrs. Sweet being careful guardian to you, either."

Hannah could feel her mouth thin into a stubborn line. "Granddad McNaughton always wanted me to advance in math," she reminded. "He even sent away for information about that special school in Boston, remember."

Pa stopped and turned to look at her. "On account of Granddad McNaughton's health," he said, his words falling as if driven by a mallet, "he'll not be consulted by us about any of this business."

Hannah said nothing, but her scalp prickled in dread anticipation, remembering what she had told Mrs. Sweet.

They reached the gate just as the sun broke, and Homer tossed his crooked comb and preened his feathers and crowed the new day. Oh, it was all so far-fetched, anyway, she thought. The farm was all she knew. Math was a joy, but nothing to leave home for.

Inside the kitchen was filled with sweet warmth.

"Doughnuts!" exclaimed Hannah.

Ma smiled. "Thank Miss Crocker. It was yesterday's recipe. I made them with part wild clover honey and part Karo. Thought we all could use a treat this morning."

She did not want to mention Philadelphia. Ma tended to close the door on topics that unsettled her.

They sat for grace and a breakfast of boiled ham and doughnuts.

On the outside, thought Hannah as she

looked around the kitchen, this morning was the same as every morning. There was bleary-eyed Roy—likely he'd been up late, reading Krazy Kat funny papers by moonlight—and Ma moving from table to stove, stiff on her arches that troubled her during cold snaps. There was Pa and Ben sipping from their mugs of nicotine tea, home brewed from hot water and crumbled tobacco, with fresh spearmint added for taste. Coffee was scarce this year. Last year it had been opposite—enough coffee, no tobacco.

"You can never get your hands on one without bemoaning the loss of the other," Pa had said. "What you get is what you get."

But sometimes isn't there a choice? Hannah wondered uneasily.

She'd pay a visit to Granddad McNaughton, she decided, after afternoon milking. Granddad would tell her the things that she needed to hear.

7

JUMPING, JUMPING

"WHY, YOU CAN hardly bumble through the *Stepping Stone* primer, Hannah. How will you get by at a city school? Scholarship!" Betsy flicked the jump rope for emphasis. "What do your folks say?"

"They say no."

"'Course they do! *I've* been to see Philadelphia, remember," said Betsy. "Trust me, you won't fit in. And what kind of people is Mrs. Sweet, anyhow? At first, she reminded me of Mrs. Roosevelt, but then I decided no—it was only her clothes that did. I bet in person, Mrs. Roosevelt is far gentler."

Tru, who was turning the opposite end, pounced to Hannah's innermost fear. "Besides, you'd be terrible with homesickness. Wouldn't you, Hannah?"

Just then, Margaret tangled in the rope. "Oh, please, let me try . . ." she began, but was over-ruled in a shriek of *no*s to the end of the line.

"My turn!" Hannah shouted. She jumped into the rope and began to sing.

How many mules from here to Mile-a-bry?
Threescore and ten!
Can I get there by candlelight?
Yes, if your legs are long, you might.
Watch out! Mighty bad witches on the road tonight!
Count one, count two, count three, count four . . .

Usually, Hannah loved this rhyme, but today

it seemed to shout a warning. A warning that echoed what Pa had said. She had never traveled off the farm alone. Only occasional trips into town for back-to-school supplies at Nutley's and a few times to the movies, once to see *Babes in Toyland* with Laurel and Hardy, once to see *Little Women* with gorgeous Katharine Hepburn starring as Jo March. And last month—after begging her folks, who gave in only because it was Melinda Snow's thirteenth birthday and because everyone else was going and because the Snows were Methodist, after all—to watch *The Gay Divorcee* with Ginger Rogers and Fred Astaire.

Movies were Hannah's favorite entertainment in the entire world. She speculated how far city folk lived from the cinemas. Walking distance, hadn't Mrs. Sweet mentioned? Her own curiosity surprised her, like swallowing snow, a mild slip-sliding shock. She shut her eyes and let the counting take over. "Thirty-two, thirty-two, thirty-two!" She always counted thirty-two a few extra skips, for luck.

"Boy, oh, boy, I'd give my eyeteeth to spend a month in Philadelphia with all those swells and bon tons," said Tru.

"My folks'd never let me," snapped Betsy. "It's fine and all to visit—like I did—but cities is full of none but thieves and thieving!"

Then other girls in the line chimed in, each voice lifting to deliver its story.

"You'll have to be on watch for falling bodies. One bad day in the stock market, and business-men start jumping out of windows—"

"I heard society ladies wear dresses made out of thousand-dollar bills and dance on top of—"

"My pa says crooks park their yachts near South Street seaport and sell black-market meat to anyone who—"

"Forty-four, forty-five, forty-six, forty-seven!" Hannah listened only to the rope. She jumped and counted and her heart pumped its blood-beat, faster and faster in her chest.

"Hannah, you can't leave Chadds Ford!" Betsy cried finally. "No place is better than here.

Besides, you and Tru and me already planned to
be June brides and live down the road from one
another. In white houses with wisteria and morning glory climbing up the lattice. My house will
have green shutters and Tru's will have red shutters and yours will have blue shutters! Like we
planned, Hannah!"

"She's not listening," said Tru. "She'll make
it be her turn forever. Show-off!"

Hannah kept jumping. Perhaps she was a
show-off, but jumping was delightful, like running and counting, and she felt as though she
could stay in motion forever. Even after the other
girls got tired and raised the rope and sped the
rope and complained that their wrists ached,
even then Hannah bet she could keep up with it,
and outlast them all.

8

CHEESE, SARDINES, AND GRANDDAD MCNAUGHTON

HANNAH SPIED Granddad outside on his front-porch rocker, chewing a plug of tobacco while he watched the last gold of sun slip off the fields. His hair was combed to cottony floss, and he was impeccably dressed in green twill pants, a waistcoat over his starched white shirt and a shine on his boots. Buttoned and pressed as usual, though the new tremble in his fingers made knotting knots and looping loops a time-eating hindrance.

But that was typical of Granddad McNaughton. He was set in his ways. Stingy with his affection, too. Certainly there was precious little of it for Ma, Pa, Hepp, or Roy, which made Granddad's fondness for Hannah seem as indulgent and quirky as a plumed hat on a monk's head.

"He loves you best because you're just like him," Roy groused to her once. "For Granddad, seeing you is the same as looking in a pond, like old Narcissus."

When Granddad spied her, he leaned down to the split of watermelon at his feet, scooped up a chunk, and winged it for Hannah's catch.

"You missed her by minutes, that dratted Mrs. Sweet," he said. "She wants to take you away in her monstrous car. Didn't like the look of her, no indeed, and so I didn't offer her one twist of my chew."

Hannah scrutinized her grandfather as she bit into the sweet end-of-season fruit. Delicious. She sat on the porch step. "Then you think I ought to stay here, Granddad? Is that what you're saying?"

"Stay here? Not on my will! Why, you're as natural to math as sparks fly upward, Hannah Bennett. I've been shouting it for years." Granddad's smile turned to a cackle, and then to the rasping cough that had plagued him all summer. Hannah waited for it to subside. "How can you ask me such a foolish question?"

"Because Ma and Pa want me home. They worry for my reading problem. And for my safety in a city."

Granddad's thistly brows knit. "That so? And do they worry for your life wasted, boiling and baking and milking and pickling away all your days here simply because you can't comprehend the sports page?"

Hannah laughed. "You make it sound too simple, Granddad. But you know we can't afford to lose one more body off the farm, not with Hepp gone. Hiring Ben's been an expense enough." She cast an eye on her grandfather, who kept his own face expressionless. "I know an opportunity like this has been a dream of yours. But I can't figure out if it's a dream of mine."

Granddad McNaughton spat over his shoulder. "Doubt on every color of the rainbow if you like, but we also both know what's what. That's why you steered Mrs. Sweet in my direction. I got stuck in Chadds Ford because nobody pushed me forward." When he opened his eyes, their pale blue light had become twin embers of anger. "A country doctor. What I could have been! No, you need to learn to speak math with people who are fluent in it. You'll rust out here, Hannah. You're rusting already."

Hannah listened, though she had heard this speech a hundred times before. "I want to go and I don't. I'm curious, but confused," she admitted.

"Bah!" Granddad retorted. "Curiosity expands us. And the way Mrs. Sweet explained it to me, if you get that scholarship, it sets you on a road that might even lead to a university education. Think of it, Hannah!"

She nodded as her fingers tapped a pattern on the porch step. To Granddad, curiosity and knowledge were all that mattered.

"Wipe that frown off your face a minute. I've got a riddle for you!" Granddad grinned. "If Hannah May Bennett opens her math book and finds that the sum of the facing pages was two hundred forty-one, what pages did she open to?"

"Pages one twenty and one twenty-one," Hannah answered promptly. She spit a watermelon seed in a perfect arc. "That's too easy. Here's one for you. Of fifty people at a picnic, forty-one like sardine sandwiches, thirty-five like cheese sandwiches, and thirty like both. How many like neither cheese nor sardines?"

"That would be . . . four. Four remaining." Granddad answered. Then he slapped his knee. "Aha, four. Your ma, your pa, Hepp, and Roy. I don't know how it is those four can't get a taste for either of our favorite sandwiches. And everyone knows that cheese and sardines are delicious together, too. Now scat, Hannah. Tell your folks they need to pay me a visit. Tell them I want a word."

"Yes, sir." She tossed the watermelon rind into the box hedge, then stood and pecked Granddad's cheek. Yet it seemed to her that she left holding the same bag of troubles she'd arrived with. All that Granddad had made clear was his own opinion, as usual.

Ma was waiting for her at the crossroads. "Mrs. Sweet paid us another visit," she said. "Seems she found a backer in your grandfather."

"I'm sorry, Ma," said Hannah. "I really, truly am. I've been wild and sleepless with sorry. But it seemed only fair that this be Granddad's business, too. I couldn't stay quiet."

Ma shook her head. "What sort of nature do you have, Hannah, to go behind-hand against your parents?"

Hannah swallowed hard. The right answer did not rise easily. "This is what Granddad's always wanted for me. How could I keep it from him, especially with him feeling so low these days?"

"Your grandfather . . ." Ma began, and Hannah was sure that Ma was on the verge of recollecting a story about her own youth, and Granddad's remote parenting, the solitary hours he'd spent in his study, more preoccupied with work than family.

But she didn't. "Thirteen years old," she said instead. "And here I thought Hepp was young to leave home at eighteen." Her voice sounded small, defeated. Family meant everything to Ma, and for a moment Hannah wanted to throw her arms around her mother and tell her it was all just a lark, because of course she would never leave, of course she wouldn't run away to Philadelphia simply on account of math. Math! Why, there was plenty of math right here in Chadds Ford. No, she did not have to go all the way to the city to get a proper math education.

But even as Hannah thought it out, she knew it was not true. There was scant more math that Miss Cascade, or even Granddad, could teach her anymore.

"I can always come back home," Hannah said, "if things don't work out. But at the very least, I owe Granddad a try."

Ma nodded, and they walked home in silence, uprooting bunches of watercress along the stream that marked their way. Boiled watercress was not as tasty as it was filling, but a quantity of salt and black pepper and butter made it bearable.

When Ma spoke again, she was all business. "In Philadelphia, you'll need to find a church to restore your faith come Sundays," she said. "And promise you won't listen to radio muck like *Amos 'n Andy*. Nor any of those haunted-house programs, either, that you and Tru love." She stopped to tug free a bunch of watercress, shaking rocks and soil from its roots. "I can't conjecture how you'll take to that city. You had better know, Hannah, even if you have Granddad's support, your pa's and my blessing is mixed."

"Yes, ma'am."

"First Hepp, now you," said Ma. "I keep faith it's not for permanent, not with either of you. McNaughtons and Bennetts have lived in Chadds Ford since always."

"Of course I'll come back, Ma," protested Hannah. "I belong here."

But Ma was finished talking. Her eyes slid past Hannah to another patch of watercress and she picked her way toward it, leaving Hannah to trail behind.

9

THE VIEW FROM BLOOM

WITH THE EXCEPTION of Grand-
dad's, Hannah had nobody's full blessing. Not
even Miss Cascade's, as Mrs. Sweet had written
a letter to her stating that all of the Wexler fund-
ing that might have gone to Brintons Bridge
School now would be used toward Hannah's
semester of board and tuition.

Miss Cascade had read the letter out loud to
the class while Hannah sat hunched, her shoulders up near her ears and blood tingling in her
face. Her teacher's disappointment was worse

than the students' baffled grumbling, and Hannah felt like a crook, robbing her schoolhouse of its treasures almost by accident.

Home was hardly a relief. Roy had grown unbearable. He baited and goaded, then mocked her when she complained. "Ooh, stop it, stop it! I'm a *scholarship* girl now!" he would squeak while pressing the back of his hand to his forehead. But Hannah knew that behind it, he was hurt and sad. Roy hadn't even finished missing Hepp, and here she was, two years younger than Roy and setting off on her own. Not to mention that she was leaving him to pick up the weight of her chores. Worst for Roy, she knew, was that here was another example of Granddad singling her out, aligning Hannah to his own ambitions.

It would take some time to set things right with Roy.

The evening before her departure, Hannah paid a final visit to the Applebee farm.

"Mrs. Sweet called our telephone. She said don't pack galoshes," Tru reported. "When are

your folks getting a telephone? It's awfully con-
venient."

"Pa says it's foofaraw." Hannah looked down
at her fringed-tongue oxfords, bought just last
month for one dollar and seventy-eight cents at
Nutley's. "No galoshes? Boy, she's discouraged
me from bringing much of anything."

"I'd put dibs Mrs. Sweet wants to buy you
minks and diamonds and trick you over into a
real city girl. By Christmas, you might be the
worst kind of snob." Tru's laugh had an edge to
it. Then she reached out and squeezed Hannah's
hand. "Come into the front room and see what
the Philco man brought us today!"

In spite of all their financial strains, Tru con-
fided to Hannah that her pa had taken another
bank loan in order to purchase their brand-
new, brass-and-walnut Philco-Transitone plus
Inclined Sounding Board. The Applebees were
fancy like that, always wanting the latest, newest
things. It was almost a sickness with some people, Pa said.

"The only radio scientifically designed as a musical instrument." Hannah mimicked the advertising announcer's voice as she tripped a finger across each beveled knob. One, two, three. Three, two, one. One, two three.

"Stop your tapping. *The Witches' Tale* comes on in five minutes," Tru said. "Let's listen, but this time, Hannah, you can't act all scaredy-cat and foolish."

"I won't, I swear."

Mrs. Applebee had prepared cherry Jell-O in glass dishes, and she let the girls take their dessert out to the side-porch swing. Tru turned up the volume so that they could hear the program through the open window.

The fuzz of static soon was replaced by music, heavy and thunderous, followed by the crash of a rainstorm. Hannah shivered in anticipation. *"Skelly Oil now presents* The Witches' Tale. *Written and produced by Alonzo Dean Cole,"* intoned the announcer in his deep, spooky voice. *"Let us now join Witch Magda and her black cat, Satan."*

"Ooh, I see her! I see Witch Magda!" Hannah yelled.

"Shh, don't wreck it!" hissed Tru.

Hannah shivered and tried to keep from wriggling as she listened to old Witch Magda cooking up her usual diabolical elixirs. Horrifying! She sneaked a peek across the Applebees' dark pasture. The longer she listened, the easier she could see those hunch-backed witches. There, in the shadows, now swooping slap over the split rail!

"I've got here a potion to melt the flesh of my worst enemies!" Witch Magda cawed as Hannah listened, delirious with dread. Oh, yes, she saw those witches perfectly! Black-robed, the warts on their chins as fat as gooseberries.

She gave up. "Turn it off, oh, turn it off!" She set down her dish and jumped from the swing. Hands clapped to her ears, she sprinted off the porch, vaulting the stairs in a bound. "Let's climb Bloom!"

Bloom was Hannah and Tru's pet name for

the giant maple that grew in the Applebees' front lawn. The girls had agreed long ago that it was the most magnificent climbing tree in the world. When she reached Bloom's base, Hannah tore off her shoes and stockings, then jumped and caught the lowest branch, and swung herself up.

Tru watched a moment, before she ducked into the house to snap off the radio. When she reappeared, she was wrenching off her shoes and running to Bloom.

"It's a sorry day when all it takes is a tin-pan rainstorm and a radio actress to put you up here!" Tru clucked her tongue as she wedged herself sidesaddle into one of the branches' sturdy forks.

"I'm safe in a tree." Hannah looked up at the stars. "I like an autumn sky better than spring-time, don't you, Tru?" She pointed. "Look, there's Cassiopeia."

"And Orion, there."

"And Sirius."

"And the Big Dipper."

"I wish I knew the math of stars," said Hannah wistfully. "What energy they're made of. What makes them burn."

"The view is enough for me." Tru dropped her gaze from the sky. "Betsy and I bet you won't last a month in the city, Hannah," she said. "Who would understand you? My granny says it's only when folks have known each other since birth that we make allowances for peculiarities."

"I'm not peculiar," Hannah retorted.

"'Course you are! What with your fingers always tapping how they do, and the way you shout out whatever's in your head, whenever the mood hits!" exclaimed Tru. "There's no *polish* to you, Hannah! Oh, don't glare at me. Maybe I ought not have spoken so truthful. But, listen, I've got some luck to pass along about your precious thirty-two." She grinned. "My uncle Frank told me that you can get thirty-two pounds of starch from a bushel of corn."

"That's a good one, Tru!"

Tru smiled. "See, Hannah? It's when you've

been friends as long as us that you can find the perfect gift." She hugged herself tighter against the tree and sighed. "I do hope you meet a new friend," she added after a thoughtful moment. "Temporarily, while you're there, I mean. All it takes is one chum to make the world shrink to a comfortable size. Wouldn't you say?"

"I'd say!" Hannah agreed, though she had never given the idea much thought.

PART TWO

10

MUDTOWN

SHE HAD GROWN up hearing the whistle of this train, used by the larger dairies to transport milk from Chadds Ford to Media Junction and then on to Philadelphia. Never, though, had Hannah boarded one of the three attached passenger cars. From her seat at the window, she watched the countryside pass by. The train took its journey slow, chugging steadily to stop an interminable time, then chuffing onward again. The stations changed, but the landscape stayed the same, fields and hills dulled to dishwater

colors by the overcast sky. She pressed her forehead to the glass and kept count of the trucks
and tractors, horses and cows, barns and silos,
and the odd automobile.

In the last few minutes, the flow and curve of
the country gave way to the city outskirts of
storefronts and paved roads. Red brick and gray
stone walls appeared solid before Hannah's eyes.
That's when she stopped counting. Looked away.
Now it that was grinding and whistling to a halt,
the journey seemed all at once too quick.

Filth-adelphia, Hannah heard a man com-
plain as the train pulled to the wide, barren con-
course that was Suburban Station. She kept her
eyes on her shoes as the train stopped. Head
bowed, she stood and collected her bag, and hurried down the stairs.

Don't look up, she warned herself. Not yet.

Inside the echoing station, Hannah followed
her feet to the nearest empty bench, where she
opened her bag and reclaimed her pungent
cheese-and-sardine sandwich. When she first

had unpacked it to eat in the train, a young woman sitting opposite had wrinkled her nose and whispered something to the man next to her. Embarrassed, Hannah had hastily dropped the smelly sandwich into the bag's side compartment alongside her thermos of milk, jam crackers, kerchief, hand towel, bottle of Listerine, cake of soap, and three Q-tips that Ma had deemed necessary for an all-day trip.

Now Hannah closed her eyes and chewed hungrily. She recalled that morning's good-byes, which had been strained and brief.

"If I could spare myself, or even Roy for a day off the dairy, I'd do it," Ma had fretted. "To settle you in."

"I'll settle myself, Ma," Hannah had reassured.

From Pa: "Keep safe, be good." Pa was inclined to go gruff when he felt a loss.

And Roy had put in: "Don't get yourself hit by a runaway truck."

The memory of Hepp's departure weighed

on all of them, Hannah knew. The mood was not helped when Granddad surprised them with a visit. Short of breath and leaning hard on his mottled sycamore cane, he had presented Hannah with a brass-and-rosewood ruler. "'Hide not your talents, they for use were made. What's a sundial in the shade?'" he had quoted with a wink. "So says Poor Richard's Almanac."

"Well, *I* knew that," Roy had grumbled. "I was the one who got to be Ben Franklin."

"Make me proud, Hannah," was the last thing Granddad told her. His hand had dropped heavy as a paperweight on her head. "You're taking the chance we've both been waiting for." His tone so smug that Pa had plucked his cap from its hook and stomped outside to wait in the truck.

Now Hannah realized she was gripping the bag's handle so hard that she could feel the beginning of a welt across her gloved palm. She released her hold, unbuckled the bag, and fumbled for the ruler. She tapped it, back and forth, end to end.

"You, there. Yes, you. Are you the milkmaid I'm sent to fetch?"

Hannah looked up. A boy who looked to be somewhere between her age and Roy's was planted, arms crossed, in the space in front of her. He was shabbily dressed in a woolen jacket and an oversized cap that shaded his dark-skinned face. Italian, Hannah guessed. Or Black Irish, or something else. She stopped tapping, straightened, wiped her mouth with her fingers. Nodded yes, although she didn't like this boy's tone or being called *milkmaid.*

"Christmas!" The boy pointed. "What's that, a doctor's bag?"

"It belonged to my grandfather," Hannah said.

"And in it's all you got?" The boy reached over and hefted its weight.

"Mrs. Sweet said not to bring much." Hannah stood and gave her hand for him to shake. "I am Hannah Bennett. Are you . . . hired by Mrs. Sweet?" she ventured.

"Hired." The boy scowled. "That's called a

presumption, you dumb bunny. My name's Joe Elway."

"I didn't mean to presume," Hannah snapped back. "Just as I'm sure you didn't mean to be nasty about it."

"Well, 'scuse me, country mouse." Joe thrust the bag back into her hand. "This way to the hack stand. C'mon."

Hannah dropped her eyes to the ground. Her oxfords, fresh-polished last night by Pa, smacked the wet sidewalk, and she wished she'd worn her galoshes. Rain had flooded the gutters and laid a thin skin of mud the color of chocolate milk on the pavement. She did not look up. On a glance, the city's patterns were complex and unnatural. They confounded her.

Instead, she counted her footsteps, the cracks in the sidewalk, the gurgle of horns, how many times Granddad McNaughton's bag slapped her shin. She listened to the rain rapping the roof of her beret and she tapped a matching beat on the side of her leg.

Joe whistled through his teeth, and Hannah looked up long enough see a yellow taxicab roaring toward them. In the next moment, it splashed water all over her shoes and skirt. She shrieked and jumped back. "You did that on purpose!"

"Did not!" But Joe laughed delightedly. "A city stinks and shakes water everywhere when it gets wet. Same as a dog. Nothing you can do." He opened the passenger door.

Hannah slid into the automobile with some misgiving. She had been in her father's truck on many occasions, and gone along on plenty of jaunts in the Applebees' Ford, but never had she shared a ride with not one but *two* strangers. She steeled her eyes to her lap and wished Mrs. Sweet had come to collect her in person.

"If you'd pick your beams off the ground a minute, I can point you out some sights along the way," Joe said. He leaned up to speak to the driver. "We're going to Delancey Place, but cut us up Market Street first, wouldja, pal?" He settled back and stretched his hands behind his head. "I'm more a bus-and-trolley man myself, but Mrs. Sweet told me to show you around. Even dropped me half a buck for traveling costs, so I got to honor her squandering. She'll try to make us pals, only the truth is, milkmaid, I'm your public enemy number one. But I'll fill you in on that later."

Hannah stared ahead and said nothing. This Joe Elway was worse than any boy in Miss Cascade's class. Even worse than Elgin Winnicker, who liked to pick slugs from his mother's lettuce patch and drop them down girls' blouses.

"Here we're coming up on City Hall," Joe continued. "Look, look out the window, wouldja? See the statue on top of that building? That's Billy Penn, and no building is allowed to rise higher than his head. It's the law. Cross the street and you've got your John Wanamaker's, the department store, you must've heard of it, huh? Piece of the Renaissance in your own backyard—though

I'm more of a skyscraper fella myself. Take this one, just went up. Look, wouldja look at it!" Joe rapped the window glass. "One Penn East. Twenty-seven stories high, polychrome, designed compliments of Ritter and Shay, the best architects this city's known since Frank Furness. And if you're keen on that, you should see the Packard Building! Well, all right, then, milkmaid, if you won't give anything the up-and-down, we might as well stop wasting my time. Delancey Place, cabby. You can turn on Eighteenth."

Eighteen. Nine times two, or nine plus nine, or three times three times two, or three times six, or thirty-six divided by two. Eighteen was how many men survived the Magellan expedition. Eighteenth of April, 1906, was the day that a terrible earthquake shook San Francisco. Eighteen was powerful, and not necessarily lucky.

After a few more minutes, Joe said, exasperated, "What are ya, homesick? You're a real wet blanket, huh? Well, it's not like I'm jumping out of my socks for you, either."

Hannah bristled. Wet blanket! Joe Elway talked as if he were one of Roy's favorite Dick Tracy thugs. She smiled thinly and said nothing, but she made up her mind that she did not like him.

11

DOLL FACE

MRS. SWEET LIVED at 5 Delancey Place, in a three-story townhouse. She seemed to attract odd numbers like a magnet. Her home was grand, with a large first-floor bay window and a brass doorknocker in the shape of a sharp-eyed fox. Hannah lifted her eyes long enough to appreciate the snug street of houses peppered with lacquered black shutters and fronted with fanlights and dormers and iron-railed stoops. As she faced the front door, her fingers reached out to tap the fox's eyes. One, two. Two, one. One, two.

Joe pushed her hand away and knocked, then stepped back and shouted, "Bev-er-leee!"

From inside came a thud and a scurry and then the door was yanked open by a girl wearing a formal maid's uniform that did not quite suit her mouse-nest hair and the coltish dangle of her arms and legs.

"You know I hate it when you yell, Joe," the girl scolded. "Come in from the rain. What'd I say about an umbrella?" She nodded at Hannah. "Let me take your coat and things. Oh, not *your* coat, Joe." She yawned as she held out a hand for Hannah's wet gloves, jacket, and beret.

"Sleeping on the job, Miss Lingle?" Joe asked, tossing his jacket and cap for Beverly to catch. He winked at Hannah. "When she's not pretending to dust around here, Beverly studies piano at the Academy. She's another Sweet discovery. We're hoping for great things, ain't that right, chippy?"

"Quit it, Joe. Lucky Mrs. Sweet is up in Boston, or she'd slap you sideways for talking to me that way," said Beverly. "Cook's off, and I'm chopping carrots for a beef stew, so you'll have to play host. Take Hannah up to her room and settle her in, how about?" To Hannah, she said, "We'll make better acquaintance over supper. When I'm not so rushed and rattled."

Before Hannah could answer, Beverly bounded off. Now Hannah caught a faint smell of simmering beef. Delectable. Beef stew must be a special Sunday treat.

"C'mon," said Joe. "You bunk down the hall from me, only I got a view and you don't, but that's how the cookie crumbles, doll face. This way."

Doll face! Not even Elgin or Roy was this irritating. Hannah gritted her teeth as she followed Joe across the foyer and up the two flights of polished pine stairs. Thirty-one steps in all, another odd number. Joe's rapid-fire speech could not distract from Hannah's astonishment at the details of Mrs. Sweet's fine house; its parquet floors and papered walls and swaths of cranberry velvet window drapes that pulled back to reveal the wet world of granite and pavement below.

But Joe demanded attention. His voice was loud, and he kept pivoting to catch Hannah's eye as he spoke.

"Most scholarship huckleberries settle in with ordinary families who live outside the city. But ole Sweet likes to keep an eye on her own investments," he told her. "That's not to say we're a team. No sirree, it's me against you, and us against all the other country rubes. We test for the Wexler cabbage before the end of December.

"If you score big, you'll ride free to some fancy school, which helps the universities sit up and take notice. If you turn out to be a dope, well, that's another story. Back to the cow patch you go. Beverly's seventeen, and she's still a dope at everything but piano. She's been Sweet's pet this year, even though she flunked the last set of exams back in June. It's no secret Sweet won't board a kid longer than one semester, but

Beverly's hanging on for one more try. Full-time student in exchange for part-time scrubbing. Without Sweet, Beverly would have got the boot back to York last year. Ever been to York, Pennsylvania? No? Well, you wouldn't want to return. Here you go, end of the hall. We'll be sharing the crapper. It doesn't got a lock, so you better learn to knock." He did a short tap dance with this last sentence.

Joe was not only rude, but also vulgar, Hannah decided. She turned her back and said nothing as she pushed open the door open on a room built plain as her bedroom at home. There was an iron bed, a desk and swivel chair, a narrow wooden bureau and matching wardrobe, and a window that looked out onto a wall of bricks. The softening touches—net drapes, the water-color that hung from a tack on the wall, a fringed-shade lamp set crooked on the sunless sill—seemed to try too hard for pleasantness.

"Sharp digs, eh?" Joe's voice boomed in her ear. "Beverly's on the ground floor, in the cook's old room, since the cook is a five-day daily, but which five days depends on her whim. Beverly likes it 'cause it's easy to sneak out with her regular beau, Charlie. That's from my mouth to your ears. Say, don't you want to know how much dough there is versus kids for the Wexler fund?"

"Not really."

"Half as much."

"All right, then."

"It's you against me. Like I said." Joe lingered, whistling. He watched as Hannah took her ruler from her bag to measure and readjust the lamp so that it was centered on the windowsill.

"That'll be all, Joe, thank you," Hannah said finally.

Joe scowled, then grinned wolfishly and held out his hand, palm up. "Christmas! If you're gonna treat me like a bellhop, you might as well tip me," he said. "Make it worth my while. That is, unless you caught on how to handle your public enemy number one, milkmaid." When she didn't answer, Joe frowned, made a shallow bow, and shut the door. He was still whistling as he walked down the hall.

Alone, Hannah felt all the fear she'd been holding back come to rest in an ache behind her eyes. She walked the edges of the room, tapping each corner. No view. A watermark on the ceiling and a scent of ammonia in the air. A cheeky boy across the hall instead of Roy—who could also be taxing, but was family, at least.

On the bureau, she found a pen and pad of paper. There was a note from Mrs. Sweet on the top page, written in a wind-bent slant. She did her best to read it.

Dear Hannah,
    I (something) not to be here. Joe will (something a something something) as host. My (something) for the (something). Becca will keep you (something). I'll be home (something)! Teddy Sweet

Becca will keep you . . . Mrs. Sweet must be

referring to the little wooden doll wedged between the bed's bolster pillows.

Hannah went to the doll and picked it up. Becca was dressed in button-up shoes and a heavy gingham smock, and her yarn hair was tied in two plaits.

Was it mockery? A country doll companion for a huckleberry farm girl? Or was Becca truly meant to be a comfort?

Hannah tapped the corners of Becca's artfully sewn patch pocket, then placed her in the bottom drawer of her bureau and shut it. Whatever Mrs. Sweet's intention, she ought to realize that thirteen-year-old girls did not play with dolls.

12

NO X, BUT PLENTY LEFT OVER

NOBODY KNEW where the milk came from.

"Germantown, I s'pose," said Beverly when Hannah asked that evening. The three of them were gathered at the kitchen table for their beef stew supper. "The butter-and-egg man's from Germantown. It's top-notch, although they bring more than we need."

Hannah did not doubt it. There was too much to eat tonight. The stew contained chunks of beef, carrot, onion, and potato generous enough to cut with a fork and knife, and there was whipped syllabub for dessert. Hannah started on the beef, eating from least to greatest, and was only up to onions before she thought her stomach would pop, and yet she could not finish what was on her plate. Beverly, who seemed to be in a permanent state of hurried distraction, was also unable to finish her portion. Only Joe made everything disappear.

Afterward, watching Beverly scrape the leftovers straight into the garbage bin, Hannah was appalled to see the amount of food wasted. At the farm, anything not eaten was saved in the ice chest for the next night, or fed to the animals, or put aside for the occasional wandering tramp who knew that the X marked on the Bennetts' back door meant he could find hospitality and a warm supper inside.

There was no X on Mrs. Sweet's kitchen door. Hannah had checked. Was that because there were no hungry people in Philadelphia? She could not imagine a band of tramps ringing the bell at fashionable Delancey Place.

"Mrs. Sweet asked me to deliver you to Ottley Friends tomorrow morning," Beverly mentioned as they tidied the kitchen together, Joe having shot off as soon as he finished eating. "The school uniform—the gray jumper and middy—are hanging in your closet. We'll walk, but we ought to leave by seven o' clock prompt, and no oversleeping, please. I have a piano lesson at seven-thirty."

No oversleeping! Hannah had to roll her lips together to resist laughing. At her house, if she or Roy slept past five, they were called lazybones and got last breakfast dibs—bread heels and pan-burnt potato.

She followed Beverly as she turned off the downstairs lights and locked the doors. "It's quiet here most days," Beverly explained. "There's the radio in the pantry, but Mrs. Sweet discourages school-night listening. We each get to pick one show a week. Joe prefers *The Lone*

Ranger, of course, and I skip between *The Romance of Helen Trent* and *Lights Out*, depending if I want tears or chills."

"Is there a Mr. Sweet?"

"Died in the war. Best not to mention it. All right, we're finished here. I'm going to the parlor to practice. I'll try to play quiet so as not to disturb you, but it's Bach, so I might get carried away. Good night."

"Good night."

As Hannah reached the third floor landing, Joe's bedroom door opened, and he poked his head out. "G'night, milkmaid," he chimed, singsong. Then he made a mooing noise, stuck out his tongue, and snapped back into his room, turning the lock.

Don't provoke and you won't be provoked. That's what Ma would have said.

Politeness counts. That's what Miss Cascade would have said.

Joe Elway needed to be taught a little lesson. That's what Hannah decided. She went swiftly to her room and from her bag unearthed the tin of Miss du Fleur's Elderberry Essence hair pomade that Betsy had given her for her last birthday. She used her handkerchief to rub a dollop of it onto Joe's doorknob until it was slippery as a leg of mutton.

Serves you right, she thought.

Back in her room, Hannah unpacked and refolded and stacked or hung the few articles of clothing and personal items she had brought. She used her ruler to space her hairbrush, comb, and mirror, as well as to center the watercolor and throw rug.

Finally, she paced the length of the room thirty-two times, touching each corner for luck.

After she changed into her nightgown, brushed her teeth, and said her prayers, she slid into the too-soft bed that was not hers, and she closed her eyes against this strange new moonless space. She tapped a pattern up and down her ribs and listened to the rise and fall of her breath.

Here I am, she thought. Right where

Granddad wanted. She tried to be happy about that, but then her mind made a picture of home: of Ma reading the Robertson's seed catalog while Pa fumbled with his pipe, Roy stretched out on the hearthrug between them. The last thing Hannah heard before she fell asleep was the for-lorn *plink* of Beverly at the piano, the same piece played and broken off and taken up again. It made Hannah feel more homesick than she wanted.

13

MEETING MR. BARNABY

WHEN HANNAH opened her eyes into the soft shadows before daybreak, she needed a moment to remember. No milking, no chores. She rose and bathed quickly anyway, then struggled into the unfamiliar gray uniform. It was loose and long, with a slide fastener up the back, and its sewn-in tags read *Friendly Frocks*. Was that a shop? A catalog? The fabric was not quite flannel and not quite wool and almost itched.

Dressed, she crept downstairs to the kitchen window with her tablet and pen and waited for sunrise.

It was not a farmer, however, who appeared with the dawn, slowing his cart and dobbin to the street corner, but a young man in a gleaming white truck. MILK MEANS HEALTH! proclaimed the script along its side. The man was outfitted in a formal uniform; white suit, black-and-white-striped tie, and white gloves. He greeted Hannah at the kitchen door with a small crate of four milk bottles and a tip of his cap.

"Up early, miss."

"Good morning, sir. I was curious to know where the milk comes from."

"Why, it comes from a bottling plant, owned by the American Dairy Industry."

Hannah thought. "But surely there is a single dairy for our milk?"

"Ouch, you might have caught me, miss." The milkman raised his eyebrows. "I'm not familiar with the process from cow to doorstep. I just drive the truck. Thing is, I've only had this job three weeks." He offered his hand. "Name's Barnaby. I was in lithographs, see, before the last round of layoffs."

Hannah shook the gloved hand. "I'm Hannah Bennett, pleased to meet you. My parents run the Bennett Dairy? In Chester County? In Chadds Ford?"

"Not familiar, sorry." Mr. Barnaby's smile stayed friendly nevertheless. "Well, Hannah Bennett, I have nine streets on my route. Nine before eight, elsewise you're late. It's the rule."

After he left, his truck clattering down the cobblestones, Hannah placed the milk bottles in the electric refrigerator. She marveled at the treasury of food packed inside. Meats, hard and soft cheeses, bottles of juice, paper packets of thin-sliced smoked fish, Hellmann's real mayonnaise, a tub of fresh horseradish, another of champagne mustard. Where did it all come from? Who made it? How much did it cost?

Apparently, none of that seemed to matter to Philadelphians. As long as it arrived on time, as long as it was fresh for the taking.

14

TOO LONG AND WRONG

FROM HER FIRST step inside the school, Hannah saw that Tru had been right. Ottley Friends girls *were* different. Graceful and glint-eyed, they called to Hannah's mind a throng of Siamese cats. In their sleek company, Hannah felt as scraggly as Mouser. As soon as she had walked through the door, she wanted to turn around and run.

For one thing, not one single girl wore a shoulder-length hairstyle. Blunt bobs and flips and pageboys were all Hannah saw as Beverly guided her up the broad stairs to Miss Jordan's office. A few of the older girls even wore finger-wave marcels. Movie-star styles, all of them! Hannah thought. She herself might as well have arrived in grosgrain-ribboned plaits, like poor Becca, for all she felt her difference.

If that weren't bad enough, her *Friendly Frocks* hemline dropped a good three inches lower than everyone else's. Between the extra length of hair and extra length of dress, Hannah felt over-burdened, a sensation similar to last night's when she had gone to bed on a too-full stomach.

"Welcome, welcome," greeted Miss Jordan, the school headmistress, in whose care Beverly had dropped her before dashing to her piano lesson. Miss Jordan was a cheerful, energetic package of a woman whose office window was filled with jeweled glass lamps and fern sprays in glazed pots. "This must seem odd to you—a townhouse school. But it's really very simple. There are five floors, with our dining hall on the fourth floor, and our overnight boarders on the top. The girls take elocution and calisthenics in the ground floor theater.

"Mrs. Sweet has told me both of your abilities in math and of your struggle with reading. We want you to make great strides in both subjects here. Mr. Cole is an excellent math teacher, and I'll be supervising your reading lessons myself. Don't you worry, Hannah. We'll get you spit-and-polished for the scholarship!"

Hannah returned Miss Jordan's informal smile, but was privately vexed. She had been half-hoping that the Ottley girls did not know about her scholarship, and that she might slip into the school day posing as an exotic niece or cousin of Mrs. Sweet's.

But Helene Lyon, the snub-nosed, swan-necked girl Miss Jordan had entrusted to guide Hannah through her first week, quickly set her straight.

"My parents generally believe in education reform to help others less fortunate," Helene said right off. "We hope you find that Ottley Friends is a honey of a school. And let me say, we're all charmed to bits that you have this opportunity."

Hannah scowled and averted her eyes. It was one thing to have Mrs. Sweet talk about Hannah's opportunity, but it was quite another to hear about it from a girl her own age. And how exactly was she "less fortunate" than Helene? Perhaps Helene was tactless to everyone. She certainly seemed like a fool, from the way she carried on.

"Ooh, what a nifty little bag, Bethany!" Helene cried as she and Hannah progressed down the hall. Or, "Say, Ruth Ann, I saw you on Pearl Street yesterday in that positively chic fox-collar coat. Is it from Strawbridge's?" Or, "Lillian Shay! I want the latest on your lunchtime tête-à-tête with you-know-who!" Helene was so interested in what the other girls had seen or done or purchased over the weekend that she often forgot to introduce Hannah.

"Oh, boy! Silly me!" she would exclaim,

touching her fingertips to Hannah's shoulder. "Ruth Ann, Bethany, Lillian. This is Hannah Bendel. Don't you remember? Miss Jordan gave us a lecture about her last week?"

"Bennett," Hannah corrected, as the girls smiled and looked at her in the charitable way that one might regard a child's painting.

"Pleased to meet you, Hannah," they would chorus, then return to whatever they were doing. Pleased to meet her and pleased to leave her utterly alone.

By lunchtime, Hannah felt her smile start to hurt, as if she had borrowed it from somebody else and it did not fit.

"Miss Jordan told us you live on a dairy farm," said chubby, blond Lillian Shay, when the girls had gathered at the long table for a lunch of cold chicken and fruit.

"That's right," Hannah answered.

"Do you have to touch smelly cows?" asked Helene. She wrinkled her nose as if a terrible smell had been placed under it.

"How else are they going to be milked?" Hannah scoffed.

"Eww," squealed Lillian with a shiver. "I could never!"

"You seem to enjoy the butter and cream," said Hannah. She made a show of looking Lillian up and down. "Maybe a cow wouldn't want to touch you, either!"

"Oh, so rude!" sniffed Lillian, a blush blotting her cheeks. "Manners must be in short supply on your farm."

"Hannah, why do you keep tapping your fingers under the table?" Helene's friend Ruth Ann pointed accusingly. "You were tapping this morning, during Chapel. It's really quite distracting."

"Don't sit next to me, then," Hannah snapped. She did not mean to say it. Her mouth was going its own way, blurting things in a terrible fashion.

"Why, I wouldn't sit next to you on a dare." Bethany shook her pageboy flip so that a lock of hair fell over her eye. "You rude thing."

"Stop it, girls," said Helene. "It's not Hannah's fault who she is, rough and uneducated." She smiled frostily at Hannah. "Some ladies are bred, other need to be taught."

Hannah clenched her fists and willed herself to silence as she finished her lunch. Tru had warned her well enough that these girls wouldn't know what to think of her. It was up to Hannah to fix her peculiarities.

Starting with a new hemline and a haircut, before the end of the week.

15

PROOFS OF OLD CODGERS

MR. COLE DID not arrive at Ottley Friends until late afternoon, when Miss Jordan had despaired that he would appear at all. According to Miss Jordan, he was punctual only when the mood took him. By then, she and Hannah had settled into Miss Jordan's office to read *Nursery Rhymes for Boys and Girls*. A baby book, Hannah fumed.

Miss Cascade had tried a similar tactic last year, but the tales of Jack Horner and Georgie Porgy hardly seemed worth reading once, let alone mucking through for hours. Also, Hannah was terrified that Helene Lyon might flounce in. Wouldn't Helene throw a giggle fit if she saw what Hannah was reading!

When the door finally did fling open, Hannah sprang from her chair like a rabbit from a trap. The nursery book thudded to the floor.

"My goodness, Hannah!" exclaimed Miss Jordan as she bent to retrieve it. Hannah forgot to apologize as she turned her attention to her new math teacher.

On a first glance, Mr. Cole reminded Hannah of the scarecrow in Ma's backyard garden patch. His graying hair poked up from his head like Homer's raggedy feathers, and his clothes seemed not to be dressing a body so much as shaping a collection of chicken-wire joints and straw parts beneath. His bushy mustache, skewed bow tie, and the blob of coffee stain down the front of his vest gave him a look of someone who had decided on an academic appearance, but then forgot to maintain it.

"Pythagorean theorem?" he asked, swiveling to stare oddly at Hannah. His right eye darted like a silvery green fish, while the left one seemed to fix onto a nonplace just past her. "Glass," he said matter-of-factly. "Sometime I'll pop it out and show you. We begin with Pythagoras. Have you got to him yet?"

When Hannah shook her head, puzzled, a smile lifted Mr. Cole's mustache. "Oh, beautiful. Proofs, proofs, proofs are beautiful! I'll show you. Come along, come along."

Miss Jordan waved an encouraging good-bye as Hannah stumbled after Mr. Cole, who was walking at a clip.

"Coffee?" he asked over his shoulder. Students jumped out of his way, giggling, though Mr. Cole himself never broke stride.

"Um, no, thank you."

"Coming through, coming through!" sang Mr. Cole. "Keep up with me, Hannah! Mathematics is changing all the time."

He led Hannah up three flights of stairs, down

a narrow corridor, and into a tiny classroom that seemed to be all his—judging from the clutter on the desk and in the bookshelves. He motioned for her to sit at a front desk, then he spun on his heel twice before he located a piece of chalk, which he used to draw a square on the board.

Inside the square he drew a triangle.

Beneath the triangle, he wrote the equation $a^2 + b^2 = c^2$.

"I don't care if you ever learn how to spell Pythagoras or Bhaskara or Chang Tshang, Miss Bennett," said Mr. Cole. Aligned, both his real and glass eye regarded Hannah with equal seriousness. "And if any of those old codgers were alive today, I'd bet they wouldn't give a hoot, either. They'd rather have you master their proofs. You'll have questions, but try to follow along. We'll take coffee in forty minutes. I can't go too long without it. We'll start with our friend Mr. P. From this single theorem, one can devise an infinite number of algebraic proofs. For example. Let *a* equal six point two five."

6.25. The numbers appeared in Hannah's head as if inked there. She drew the first easy breath of her day. Mr. Cole's face was a study in enchantment as he prepared to dive headlong into the Pythagorean theorem, and soon Hannah could see nothing but numbers as she slipped through the door of her mind and lost herself inside.

16

SATURDAY WITH MAE

JOE SAID NOTHING about his pomade-greased doorknob, but when Hannah came home from Ottley Friends that afternoon, she found that every ruler-ordered object in her room had been set askew.

What a nuisance Joe Elway was turning out to be!

But he was not a tattletale. When Mrs. Sweet returned from Boston at the end of the week, Joe pretended that he and Hannah had made cordial introductions.

"I showed her around town, just as you asked, ma'am," Hannah overheard him say. "I think she's settled in fine."

Mrs. Sweet, after checking in on Hannah and asking her some questions about how she had settled into her school, left promptly for a night at the opera.

"You'll find Sweet hardly takes a blind bit of notice to us," Beverly explained to Hannah during dinner. "If you haven't figured out already, all she wants is for us to win scholarships so that her photograph will appear in the *Inquirer* alongside the city bigwigs, and Mayor Moore'll grant her a goodwill ambassadorship or something. What she doesn't want is for us to be pesky."

"Her sons are grown and scat, one to England and the other to California," added Joe. "I'da moved across the country, too, to get away from all that bossing."

Hannah soon determined, however, that Mrs. Sweet's presence was not so bossy as akin to a mild haunting. She was a patter of footsteps, a rattle of the tea tray, a faint burst of laughter through the air ducts of her bedroom down into the kitchen. Mostly, however, Mrs. Sweet was out. Out at ladies' lunches, or out to meet friends at the Wanamaker's eagle for a day of shopping. She often returned with purchases for Joe, Beverly, or Hannah, dropping the packages of galoshes or gloves on the table in the foyer.

"Though she never troubles to ask beforehand what any of us might need," said Beverly as she handed out new toothbrushes and socks, the spoils of one of Mrs. Sweet's excursions. "With Mrs. Sweet, you get what you get."

"Like coffee or tobacco," said Hannah.

Beverly laughed. "I guess so."

On the first Saturday after her return, Mrs. Sweet did supervise Hannah's haircut, telephoning the appointment herself and walking Hannah to her own personal beauty parlor.

"Very up-to-the-minute, Hannah," Mrs. Sweet said as she jotted the check to the hairdresser. "And here's fifty cents for lunch and a matinee. The cinema's just 'round the corner. I'm meeting some of my friends for bridge in Willow Grove. Ta!"

"Oh." Hannah had hoped this Saturday Mrs. Sweet might show her some of the city's sights— maybe even the Bellevue-Stratford Hotel with its harp-playing angel. But it seemed that Beverly was right; Mrs. Sweet was not prepared to take a blind bit of notice.

Disappointed, Hannah watched Mrs. Sweet's jaunty beret dissolve among the throng of caps and cloches. All around her, the city bustled, moving swiftly on its various joints and hinges. If only Granddad were here, she thought. He would know the right way to spend the after-noon. He would know where to take her.

Hannah stared at the quarters in her palm. Fifty cents was a stupendous amount of money. All she ought to be was grateful. She clutched the coins as she made her way dutifully to the cin-ema, where she lined up for her ticket among the sweetheart couples and family clusters. The fingers of her one hand tapped up and down the newly exposed nape of her neck while the other gripped her two quarters.

The new W.C. Fields film, *It's a Gift*, was playing. But on a last-minute impulse, Hannah bought a ticket to see *I'm No Angel*, starring Mae West. With thirty-eight cents left over, she decided to spend another nickel on a packet of jelly babies.

It was at the counter that she heard the voices.

"See her there? Up in front. Her hair's changed."

"Where? Oh, I see."

Helene Lyon and Lillian Shay! And they were talking about her! Hannah stopped tapping her neck and plunged her hands into her pockets, forcing herself not to turn around while her ears pricked up to eavesdrop on their prattle.

"How odd for Miss Tippity-tap to attend the cinema by her lonesome," remarked Helene.

Lillian sniggered. "Well, it's not as if she can

spend the afternoon browsing in a bookshop or library!"

"Poor thing," said Helene lightly. "I suppose I could lend her some of my baby brother Dixie's picture books. He's got no need for them since he started kindergarten."

"Oh, reading's only one of Miss Bennett's afflictions," said Lillian. "If she gets that scholarship, it'll be nothing short of robbery."

Then they *did* know! And Hannah had thought she had kept her reading a secret. Blushing hotly, she made her request to the candy-counter girl, and squared her back against Lillian and Helene as she hurried into the theater. She chose a seat in the last row and wriggled all the way down in it so that the girls would not see her when they trotted past. Miss Tippity-tap—what a mean nickname! If only she had a couple of Elgin Winnicker's garden slugs on hand!

The lights darkened, and she tried to shake the girls, and their insults, from her mind.

Luckily, the newsreel was brief and was followed by two childish but funny Donald Duck shorts. And Mae West was divine, like a glittery, friendly witch. It was only after the magic was over and the lights were brought back up again that Hannah remembered about Helene and Lillian.

She watched as the pair swept out through the front exit. Good riddance, she thought as she crept out the back, although she couldn't help but wonder where the girls were off to.

No, I'd rather be alone than with them, she thought. Even if alone means lonely.

As it was, the rest of Saturday afternoon loomed. No chores, no afternoon milking, no helping Ma with pitting peaches or ironing sheets or waxing floors and furniture. Hannah followed her feet to the vendor's cart on Front Street, where she bought a soft pretzel with an extra spatula swipe of mustard. From another peddler, she bought a pickled egg. She ate with her chin tucked rather than witness the city speed along too fast. She could never find order in its patterns. If she counted a blockful of cars or people, by the next minute, the number had changed.

It was past dinnertime when Hannah arrived at 5 Delancey Place. The house was dark. In the pantry she found a covered plate of baked apples and lamb chops. Nobody was waiting up to reprimand her, or to hear of her adventures, or to express relief that she had found her way home at all. From the parlor came the *plink-plink* of Beverly practicing scales. From everywhere else, silence.

17

DINNER AT DELANCEY PLACE

"Command performance!" Mrs. Sweet bellowed as she pushed through the kitchen door the following Friday morning, startling everyone because traditionally she took breakfast on a tray in her room. "I've got a dinner party tonight, and I expect you *all* here. Very important people will be in attendance. First, Hannah will do her numbers tricks; then Joe will recite, with Beverly's music in the parlor to close. Yes, you, Joe!"

Joe stared glumly into his bran mash, but he did not protest.

"Settled? Splendid. You'll eat in here as usual, and I'll summon you during cheeses."

After Mrs. Sweet left, Joe stuck his tongue at the door. "No better than an organ grinder's monkey," he said. "I'm gonna ask her if I can get paid for this stint."

"Are you really?" asked Hannah.

"Sure I'm really!"

Hannah could not tell if Joe Elway was joking. Day to day, she did not see or speak to him much. His school was on Girard Avenue, north of the city and a long bus ride from Delancey Place, and he was crabby most mornings, besides. In the afternoons, he stayed in his room, and when he wasn't there, he kept the door locked and wore the key on a frayed bootstrap looped around his neck, a reminder that he treasured his privacy.

In truth, Hannah had not worked hard for Joe's friendship, either. After he'd played the trick of rearranging her room, she had hidden two chunks of broiled cod in each of his galoshes that he'd left to dry at the kitchen stove. The next day, she'd seen him scrubbing his boots out in the washtub, using bleach to kill the stink.

He never said a word, but he never tattled on her, either.

Joe Elway would have fit in at Brintons Bridge School, thought Hannah. He understood the code of pranks.

She was reminded of this later that morning at school during morning assembly, when she opened her hymnal to find a drawing of a girl sitting astride a cow. Out of the girl's mouth was a bubble that read: *A B C and 1 2 3. Looky here, Maw, I kan reed 'n cownt togethar!*

From all around her, Hannah heard the twittering laughter of Lillian and Ruth Ann and, of course, Helene. Her fingers gripped the edge of her hymnbook so as not to start tapping. That would only make the girls giggle more. She flipped the hymnal to the correct page, stuck up her chin, and sang "In Your Glory, O God, I Take Refuge" extra loud. Instead of tapping, she blinked her eyes along with the hymn's meter.

That picture wasn't funny, Hannah thought unhappily. It was *mean*. There was a difference.

At lunch, Ruth Ann passed out her Halloween party invitations. Hannah pretended indifference when she did not receive one. No matter how hard she tried not to notice, she spent the rest of the afternoon spying the creamy-white envelopes. Some of the girls made it a point to keep a corner peeking out of their uniform pockets for all to see.

Mean.

Hannah wondered if back home, Frank Dilworth might be planning his own annual Halloween pumpkin-carving party. Frank Dilworth, who gave out his invitations simply by standing upon a chair and announcing it to the entire class.

By the time school let out, Hannah had forgotten all about Mrs. Sweet's dinner party. It was a surprise to return to 5 Delancey Place and find the house scented with silver polish and lemon wax and the papery freshness of cut roses, and to see Mrs. Sweet herself standing in the hall, gossiping on the telephone. "Oh, my, yes . . . and it didn't help that he smashed up two flivvers in a month . . . Imagine, a man of his age, stepping out with that Strickland girl. . . . Darling, it's unspeakable!"

Mrs. Sweet could hold a line forever. Hannah had never known anyone to use a telephone in such a way. Pure frippery, Pa would say.

Without breaking the flow of her chatter, Mrs. Sweet handed Hannah a letter postmarked from home. A quick glance at the handwriting and Hannah knew it was from Betsy. Hannah grinned and raced upstairs to her bedroom to enjoy it in private. Even in Betsy's round, easy print, the words came slow.

Last Saturday, all bodies keen and able arrived at school and fixed that roof. 'Bout time! Miss Cascade is getting hitched to

Wendel Nutley, but she won't come out and say. Frank's Halloween party is this Saturday next and Tru's got a dear new twinset in a cherry print—lucky child! I'm wearing my same navy.

Tru had printed in the postscript.

P.S. 'lo, Hannah! A new one for you: Thirty-two is the F° at which water freezes. We miss you dearly! Tru.

Hannah folded the letter and placed it in her top drawer with her various other notes, most from Ma and Pa and Granddad and Roy, and even a bulletin from Hepp that Ma had forwarded on. *You'll be home in a month,* Tru had predicted. And now a month had passed, and it seemed to Hannah that home was the only place in the world where she wanted to be.

18

THE VOICE OF ULYSSES

SOON HANNAH heard cab doors slam and shouts of greeting as guests began to arrive for Mrs. Sweet's dinner party. By the time she had readied herself and joined Beverly and Joe in the kitchen for supper, the parlor was alive with conversation.

Like Hannah, Beverly wore her Sunday best, but Joe was defiantly dressed in his regular school clothes, his precious key dangling like a charm around his neck.

"Mrs. Sweet has invited a heap of people," said Beverly. "I'm sure they'll gum it up all night." She stifled a yawn. "And tomorrow the house'll need a tips-to-tails cleaning, with cigar ash and wine spills everywhere! There goes my morning practice!"

As guests trickled into the dining room, Hannah heard Mrs. Sweet's bellow as she rearranged place settings. Millicent and Roseanne, two sisters who were friends of Beverly's from the Academy, had been hired for the evening. They stepped quickly back and forth from kitchen to dining room, carrying out the heavy serving plates. Voices became more boisterous as the night wore on.

"I haven't much experience with crowds," Hannah said. She took a last bite of roast beef and moved clockwise to her sweet potato, swallowing hard past the fear that stuck in her throat.

"There's nothing to experience here except hungry academics and boring chumps who come for the filet." Joe slurped his milk and banged down the empty glass. "Most people with their heads stuck on straight think Teddy Sweet is the dopiest dame in a dope pack."

Beverly grinned. "That's not true. Maybe we're the dopes."

"Naw. Tonight, Bev, we're the organ grinder's monkeys," said Joe. "I ought to have dressed as a clown or a doorman."

Millicent and Roseanne, slouched in tipped-back chairs by the stove, were using their between-courses break to smoke cigarettes and drink Pepsi-Cola mixed with a splash of kitchen sherry. "Give us a jingle, Joe," prompted Millicent. "If you're in a mood to entertain."

Immediately and in a creaky voice Joe jumped up and sang, "'Leprosy! You've got leprosy! Was that your eyeball that fell into my highball?'" Even Hannah joined in the laughter as Joe scratched his head and sides and hopped around the kitchen. The sound of the buzzer stopped him. "You're up to bat, milkmaid," he announced. "I'll go out with you."

The dining room was layered blue with smoke and was thick with the scent of steak as Hannah entered, Joe at her side. She blinked.

There were the Baltzells, the Austins, and the Klines, all friends of Mrs. Sweet's whom Hannah had met before, as well as a few people she'd never seen. One guest struck her eye immediately. He was a young colored man, smooth-cheeked as a girl, with toffee-colored eyes so wide-set it seemed that he could look around and at her at the same time.

"*This* is my little math ward, Dr. Claytor," said Mrs. Sweet, addressing the man. She was enthroned at the head of the table, wearing enough diamonds, Hannah figured, to start her own pawnshop. To Hannah, she said, "Dr. Claytor has just earned his Ph.D. in mathematics from the University of Pennsylvania. He is publishing his thesis on . . . oh, darling, help me! I can't even pronounce half the words!"

Dr. Claytor smiled. "'Topological Immersion of Peanian Continua in a Spherical Surface,'" he answered.

There was some laughter. "Twenty-six years old, and a future as bright as the sun," remarked gruff Mr. Kline. "Nothing to stop you, William."

Dr. Claytor inclined his head in acceptance of the remark. "Perhaps nothing, Donald," he countered, "and then again, perhaps our good friend, Dr. Robert Lee Moore."

"Now, but we mustn't ruin our party with talk of such hostile things!" retorted Mrs. Sweet. She clapped her hands together. "Not when Hannah has this wondrous trick. Now, dear, count some letters in the first five pages of *Light in August*. It's on the butler's table. Awful novel, *I* thought. Vulgar Southerner! Dolores, you pick the letter, so you know it's not been fixed beforehand."

"The *b*s," said Mrs. Kline.

Guests turned their attention to Hannah. Alarm swept her in a wave from head to toe. She did not feel confident under the attention. She wished she could be more like Roy, who had given such swagger to Benjamin Franklin. Quickly, she tapped the book's hardcover corners. Then flipped the first five pages and scanned the bs. "Ninety-seven."

"No, no! Impossible!" Mrs. Kline held out her hand for the book. "How could you see them all so fast?"

While Mrs. Kline took the book and recounted, Hannah answered some simple word problems that Mr. Kline made up about apples and grasshoppers.

Then Mrs. Kline held up the book and exclaimed, "Ninety-seven, exactly!"

There was some scattershot clapping, and Hannah was finished. She stepped back from the table. When no one was looking, she crossed her eyes and stuck out her tongue at Joe. Ha—let's see you top ninety-seven bs, she thought.

Mrs. Sweet called on Joe to recite. "Anything! As long as it's an important person!"

"Tennyson's 'Ulysses'?" asked Joe. "There's two important people. I'll skip the beginning and cut straight to my favorite part."

Mrs. Sweet nodded and swooped a conductor's finger for him to start.

"'I cannot rest from travel,'" Joe began. His voice was clear and calm. "'I will drink life to the lees. All times I have enjoyed greatly, have suffered greatly, both with those that loved me, and alone.'" Without pause or falter, Joe stepped into the role, becoming the old hero, Ulysses. No mugging, no hamming, as Joe made Ulysses' troubles come alive, transporting Hannah to a world even more vivid than Miss Cascade had ever brought to her schoolroom.

After he finished, the table sat silent, spellbound, until Mrs. Sweet broke the mood with a ping of her spoon on her wineglass.

"Thank you, Hannah and Joe," she said. "You may go now."

"Hold up, Joe. Do you know any Eliot?" asked Mr. Baltzell. "'Prufrock', perhaps?"

"Sure do," Joe answered, holding out his palm. "You got a penny for it? I *am* a professional, after all. Need to earn my keep."

Now that, Hannah thought, was most certainly rude. Her fingers began to tap the cover of *Light in August* as the room went silent. Mrs. Sweet's eyes widened, and her jaw dropped. She looked to Hannah rather like a lace-wrapped trout. Mrs. Kline touched a nervous hand to her tarnished-silver curls. Then Dr. Claytor threw back his head and roared. His laughter was followed by Mrs. Baltzell's, and it wasn't long before everyone at the table was convulsed in mirth. Joe was laughing hardest of all.

Mr. Baltzell pulled out a chair and offered him the platter of cheese, which pleased Joe— although, Hannah noticed, it annoyed Mrs. Sweet.

"Yes," said Mrs. Sweet, her smile set as carefully as her centerpiece. "Both you children, sit. And when we're ready to move to the parlor, I'll get Beverly to come play a teensy sonata for us. What sharp kiddos!"

"Here, here," cried Mrs. Baltzell, raising her glass.

19

BLOWN BACK

As THE DINNER party began to break up, Beverly, Joe, and Hannah helped the guests with their coats. Hannah made sure she got hold of Dr. Claytor's. She held his hat and gloves for him as he buttoned his overcoat.

"Why are you looking at me that way, my friend?" he asked.

"I wanted to know, sir, who is Dr. Robert Lee Moore?"

"Ah, Robert Lee Moore." Without changing expression, Dr. Claytor's features seemed to harden as if glazed by an invisible frost. "The good professor is favored to become the president of the American Mathematical Society next year, and last I heard, women were discouraged from attending his lectures, and coloreds were prevented." He fell silent, giving the words their space. Then he winked at Hannah and his expression turned to flesh and blood again. "You will learn in time that while some doors are open, others are stuck and need pushing. A good strong push from one is a push for us all."

He set his hat on his head, raised it to Hannah, and replaced it. "Good night."

"Good night," she answered.

She watched as Dr. Claytor departed, leaving her to her thoughts.

While Pa and Ma had expressed a few doubts, Granddad McNaughton hardly ever mentioned the limitations of becoming a woman mathematician. Certainly at Ottley Friends, Miss Jordan and Mr. Cole did not treat Hannah as if doors were closed to her.

But of course some doors would be, Hannah contemplated. In spite of her best efforts. Dr. Curie probably had had to push against a lot of doors. She had likely seen her share of knuckleheads such as Robert Moore. If she could do it, then so can I, Hannah decided. That's what Granddad would say. Real learning was harder work than pushing against homesickness, or pretending not to care about a Halloween invitation snub or a cruel cartoon drawing.

Now Hannah envisioned Dr. Moore as another, fiercer caricature, like a storybook painting of the North Wind. Eyebrows like lightning bolts and cheeks rounded, blowing her and Dr. Claytor like seeds in the opposite direction of wherever the fields of math might lie.

It made her shiver, as if some of that wind already had puffed through her. She went to the front hall window and pulled aside the velvet drapes and watched Dr. Claytor as he strode alone down the street, past the last lamppost and into the darkness.

When she rounded the stairs to her bedroom, Hannah found Joe waiting for her, sitting at her desk as if it were his own.

"Counting letters." He snapped his fingers. "Not a bad trick!"

"Knock it off!" she said, surprising herself because this was not an expression she used. It was Mae West's, she realized. "My math teacher, Mr. Cole, says it's better than a trick," she bragged shyly. "He says some people read numbers naturally in sequences. I'm not bad at breaking codes, either."

"Christmas, a human cipher!" Joe exclaimed in a voice of genuine envy. "I'da counted you for a lost cause, but you might grab a scholarship out of my hands after all." His voice dropped, as if he were letting Hannah in on a secret. "There's fancy boarding schools that admit Wexler-funded kids, you know. That's where I aim to go. Breathe clean air again, up in New Hampshire or Rhode Island." He used his palms to launch a full swivel before facing Hannah again. "Would you head north? If you took my scholarship money, that is?" His face turned serious.

"Joe, I'm not fixing to take *your* scholarship."

"But if you did."

"I can't imagine going anywhere except close to home," Hannah confessed. "I miss home." In a blurt, she added, "I've got no friends here, see. Not that I care," she ended weakly.

"Well, who'd be your friend, bunny?" Joe's frown disappeared. "You're nobody's idea of fun. You've got no spirit. You're a wet-blankety, sulky, boring girl."

"I am not!"

"Plus, you're a snob." Joe's smile crinkled the corners of his eyes.

"A snob? I'm a snob?" Hannah blinked. "I'm not a snob!"

"Shows what *you* know." Now Joe seemed to relax. He propped his boots on the desktop, leaned back, crossed his eyes, and stuck out his tongue at her. "Not a real, born-and-bred Ottley snob. But in your own right, you're as bad as

Sweet. Wearing her clothes, eating her hash, spending her lettuce."

"I'm only trying to make the best of things." Hannah opened her door wider and stomped her foot to make Joe leave. "Shows what *you* know."

Joe didn't move, except to point a finger at her. "The best of things! Huh. Name one best thing you've done since you got to this city, milk-maid, or one thing that interests you. Besides playing the odd prank on me."

One best thing. The challenge stopped her. She thought of movies she'd seen and candies she'd eaten. She thought of the small steps she'd taken in her reading. She thought of her morning chats with Mr. Barnaby. She thought of the new music program, *Fifteen Minutes with Bing Crosby*, that she and Beverly tuned into on nights when Mrs. Sweet was out. She thought of riding on the subway, the weight of the city above her head and the shake of the tracks beneath her feet.

Yet she knew that none of these things would be best enough for Joe Elway.

"What have you done so swell yourself, Mister Elway? Have you been to see the Liberty Bell? Have you drunk tea at the Bellevue-Stratford?"

"I'd say not." Joe looked indignant. "The bell's broke, and there's no fun in a bunch of tea-drinking dames. I get to places where a fella can breathe and stretch. If you don't do it regular, you go flabby. Tell you what. I don't know how you've been wasting your time—napping at the cinema and gnawing bonbons, probably. But if you're around tomorrow, I'll show you the town. You got to promise not to be a snob or a bug, though. 'Cause this'd be a favor from me to you, milkmaid. From the goodness of one guy's heart." He thumped his chest, slid up from her chair, and, whistling, walked past her. "'Night, then."

She said good night and shut the door, puzzled. Was Joe serious?

And was she really all of those things Joe said—sulky, snobby, boring? Could it be that some of her difficulties did not lie inside this house or school, or even in Philadelphia, but inside herself?

The thoughts chased through her mind as she prepared for bed, only to find that Joe had short-sheeted it.

20

ALUMINUM CITY

THE NEXT MORNING, Hannah had finished breakfast and was staring out the bay window. Waiting for Joe, though she might have denied it if asked.

Suddenly, she spied him outside walking toward Eighteenth Street. His cap was pulled low and his hands dipped deep in his coat pockets. He must have seen her and decided to sneak out the back door! Well, he wouldn't get off that easy.

"Wait up!" Hannah called, rapping on the window. She dashed for her coat on the way out the door and caught up, breathless, at the end of Delancey. "Where are you going? You said you'd show me the town today! I want to stretch my legs!"

"Aw, quit yawping." Joe looked her up and down. "If you're serious, you better know my day runs different from yours, milkmaid. From stem to stern."

"That's fine. I still want to come along." She shadowed Joe he strode around the back alley. From behind a horse trough, he kicked forward a skato.

"My escape vehicle," he told her.

Hannah had not known Joe owned a skato, though she had seen lots of boys riding them since she'd arrived in Philadelphia. Even back in Chadds Ford they were the fashion. Roy had built a skato for himself, using a pair of wheels pried off his outgrown roller skates, a piece of board, and an orange crate. But it hadn't worked on the dirt roads, and had collapsed into pieces when Roy tried to jump it off a homemade ramp he'd built from a stack of stripped truck tires.

Joe's skato looked nicer than Roy's, Hannah had to admit. It was sleek and narrow instead of box-sided, and was painted blue, with rubber-padded T-shaped handlebars.

"I built it with scrap-yard parts and added an extra set of wheels," Joe said proudly. "That's why it's strong enough to carry extra junk. Or an extra person." He straightened the wheels and stepped on. "Hold me around the side and push off with your right foot when I say go."

Hannah faltered. "You want me to ride with you on that?"

"Look, like I was saying, you better not be a snob or a bug about—"

"I won't!" She stepped onto the skato and held Joe's waist firmly. "I'm ready."

On Joe's "One-two-three—go!" and a strong push, they shot down the alley.

"Lean into my turns and keep your eyes up, not down watching your toes grow," Joe said. "I've seen the way you walk, milkmaid. We're hooking a left on Sansom."

Hannah squinted, enjoying the sun and the numbing breeze on her face. Buildings slipped past at a clip as the paving bumped beneath her shoes.

"'Scuse me! Coming through!" called Joe.

A car honked for them to move to the side. "Gee, buddy, there's room for us all!" Joe scowled, raised and shook his fist. "Curse it, but automobiles think they own these roads!"

"Where are we going?"

"On a mission."

"For what?"

"For aluminum."

"Aluminum?" Hannah laughed. "Why?"

"'Cause once we get enough, we'll sell it to Mr. Lee, the rag and junk man. He buys everyone's old scrap iron and aluminum, even newspapers. Twelve cents a pound is what he'll pay for metal. You can sweep in an easy couple of dimes, good clean money, if you know how to look."

Hannah leaned with Joe as they made a right

onto Sansom Street. Almost immediately, and
with a triumphant "Aha!" Joe braked. He
hopped off the skato, nearly upsetting it, ran
halfway down the street, then leaned over and
picked something off the road. He jogged back
holding a twist of aluminum between his fingers,
which he crushed into a ball and tossed for
Hannah's catch. "Keep the goods in your coat
pocket. I got a sack for when we start hauling.
Just you watch how this adds up."

She dug her fingers into Joe's overcoat pockets as they continued up Sansom, Joe whistling
passersby out of their path. A glint caught
Hannah's eye.

"Stop! I see something!" she cried. Once Joe
set his foot on the pavement, she jumped off the
skato and ran to where an empty box of cigarettes was lying inches from the gutter. She bent
to retrieve it, then unpeeled the sheet of foil from
the thin paper and held it high for him to see.

Joe pointed. "And there's two more packs in
that trash can there. Get 'em."

It only took a moment's deliberation before Hannah nodded, rucked up the sleeve of her wool coat, leaned over, and dug through the garbage bin until she had grasped hold of both empty cigarette packs. She unstuck the aluminum foil and mashed it with the other pieces into a silver ball the size of a plum. They would need to find lots more aluminum to weigh in a pound, she figured.

The adventure was what counted, though, and Philadelphia seemed almost friendly with Joe in it. He talked Hannah through its sights just as he had that first rainy afternoon. Which didn't seem quite so terrifying today, perhaps because not only did Joe know places, he knew people. Tony the ice man. Mrs. Oppenheimer, who made and sold boxed Japanese gardens on the corner of Sansom and Fourth. The skato gang: Si and Marshal and Francis, who were lingering in the doorway of the butcher shop, hoping for pocket money by delivering meat to houses and restaurants.

"Hullo, Joe!" said Francis, steering his yellow-striped skato in a slow circle around them. "Whaddaya know? Gonna introduce us to your sweetheart?"

"She's no sweetheart. This is only Hannah," said Joe. "You know I got a girl already. Ole Hannah's helping me collect aluminum."

"Saw some lucky bird haul a whole radiator to Mr. Lee this Thursday last," Marshal told them. "Got nine dollars for it, special patriot's rate, what with Armistice Day 'round the corner. She'll be eating caviar and blinis for a month."

Joe scoffed. "We'll earn double that, the rate we're going. See ya later, boys."

It wasn't until they were on their way again, the boys gone from sight, that Hannah had to ask, "Who is your girl, Joe? I never met her."

"'Cause I don't really have one is why. But a fella's gotta say what he's gotta say, and your lips aren't smoochable enough to be any million-dollar doll face of mine."

"Joe Elway, you don't even know from smoochable!" Hannah retorted.

"Takes one to smooch one," he called over his shoulder.

They combed the city all morning, peeling their treasures from discarded cigarette packs and wheeling into some better luck with an empty tin of Bon Ami and two Campbell's soup cans that had been dropped in plain sight off the South Street wharf. Toward noon, it was Joe who spied their best prize, a muffin pan abandoned in an alleyway on Panama Street.

"That gives us five pounds, easy," said Joe, parking the skato and then dropping to sit on the curb. "We'll go around to see Lee after lunch." He pulled a squashed, waxed-paper package from his jacket and unwrapped it to reveal a lumpy sandwich. "I'll split. Cheese and mustard."

Hannah dropped down next to him. She was tired and surprised to hear her stomach gurgle. Back home, she'd always been hungry before every meal, but at Delancey Place, the food arrived before the appetite. She took the offered half of sandwich gladly.

"Say, Joe, are those boys, Francis and those fellows, are they friends of yours from school?"

Joe snorted. "I only wish! They go to Our Lady of Lourdes, where I'd wanna be, too, but it doesn't give out scholarships. My school's full of fellows so lousy with money they can't even tell what it's worth. Meantime, back home, my brothers sleep head to foot, two to a cot, and live underground fifteen hours a day."

"Underground? How's that?"

"I mean coal mines. Elways are coal men. How we all live and die, till me."

"Then how did Mrs. Sweet find you, if you were underground?" Hannah asked.

Joe rolled his eyes. "My sister Sally's to blame. She said it wasn't natural to remember things like I do, word for word, like church sermons from years ago. She thought I might have a blessing or a curse on me. I was like a joke that she couldn't decide was funny or not. This past April, Sally blew her last nickel to send me to Pittsburgh to be looked at by Monsignor Carroll. I met him all right. Recited the entire Advent, from First Kings, 'The Miraculous Rain,' Chapter Eighteen, verses one through forty, through 'The Birth of John the Baptist,' Luke One, fifty-six through eighty. And all the psalms in between."

He smiled. "Monsignor said the only thing unnatural was to allow my mind to go to waste. He fixed me up with some academic big shots. Which is how I came to meet Sweet. Sally's got different plans for me now. Wants me to invent something useful, like a flying car. A get-rich-quick-scheme, so she can drive a Ford coupe and serve oxtail consommé out of a gold tureen."

"Is that what you want?"

Joe pondered it. "Sure I'd like to help out my family, after all this educating. But I'm no money-grubber. And so far as I see, the only people who should have boatloads of cash are bank robbers. Those're the ones risking their necks. Betting on their lives. Of course, Hoover and all his men zotzed the bravest ones. Bonnie and Clyde both took their hits this past spring. John Dillinger got picked off in July, standing right outside the cinema. Heard they sold scraps of his bloody shirt as souvenirs. And Pretty Boy Floyd!" Joe sliced his hands together, brushing off bread crumbs. "He got the lead pump only last Monday, while he was holed up in Wellsville. Wellsville! Poor guy died under an apple tree. Guess you didn't read about it. And so now," Joe concluded unhappily, "all there is left is Baby Face Nelson. But Mr. Special Agent Hoover's never gonna put his cubs on *him*."

"Baby who? I never heard about a crook named Baby Face." Hannah had not heard of some of those others, either. She wondered if Joe was only teasing.

Joe turned on her, indignant. "Whaddaya talkin' about, you never heard of Baby Face Nelson? Don't you read the papers? Don't you

hear the song? 'Baby Face! You got the cutest little Baby Face.' I've cut out all his clippings for
my scrapbook. Coppers and gumshoes need eyes
in the back of their heads to catch Baby Face."

"I heard the song, but I don't read the
papers," Hannah admitted. "Can't, that is."

"Can't what?"

"Can't read. I mean, I can a little. But not a
lot. Not a newspaper's amount."

"Can't read? Ha!" Joe laughed. "For Pete's
sake, if that's not the dopiest thing I ever heard."

"It hardly bothered me back home," Hannah
confessed. "But the Ottley Friends girls aren't
as . . . *charitable* as my real friends in Chadds
Ford. Most days I'm more concerned that
Helene Lyon is spying at me through the keyhole
while I'm having my tutorials in Miss Jordan's
office."

"I guess Ottley Friends isn't so friendly to
milkmaids," said Joe. "Anyhow, you'll never get
my scholarship if you can't *read!*" He laughed,
slapping his knees. "Here I've been in a horse

sweat over the competition! Aw, get a look at that sourpuss face on you. Cripes, I'm mostly ribbing. I *know* I'll get a scholarship. I'm so sure on that, I'll teach you to read myself. First you gotta figure what you want to read. Then it's easy as fish stew." He snapped his fingers.

Hannah shrugged as if it didn't matter to her. She could never tell if Joe was being earnest. He seemed awfully confident about being able to teach her. If it was only in jest, though, she did not want to appear eager.

"Boy, oh, boy, I'd like to see you try," she said in a Mae West–ish, careless way, but she tapped a hopeful pattern on each knee before she could stop herself.

21

RITTENHOUSE WILLOW

SHADOWS HAD grown longer than their objects by the time they wheeled all the way to Forty-sixth and King Street, where Mr. Lee kept his cart parked out front of the Coal, Coke & Wood Warehouse. In exchange for their scrap metal, Mr. Lee gave Hannah and Joe twenty-three cents apiece. Hannah held the two silver dimes and three copper pennies tight in her palm.

"This is the first cash money I ever earned," she admitted. She didn't know why she was so happy about it. After all, Mrs. Sweet had tossed her fifty cents' allowance just last week! Yet Mrs. Sweet's money had made her feel guilty, and she'd spent it in a hurry. This money was different, Hannah decided. It was more important. It was *hers.*

She buttoned the coins into the inside breast pocket of her coat.

"We ought to get home." She lifted her face to the darkening skyline. "Chestnut would be quickest." It had not taken long for the grid of the city to unfold smooth as a map in her mind's eye. Its patterns were clear, even math-minded, now that she'd spent the whole day navigating. She was glad Joe had followed her suggestions when she told him the quickest way to get from here to there. Joe was not one to pretend he knew more than he did.

"Chestnut," Joe agreed. "Only first lemme show you something. Hold on."

Hannah held on and pushed off with a leg that was aching sore from the strain of use. Joe sped them downtown on Chestnut Street. When they turned onto Walnut Street, Hannah saw they were on their way to Rittenhouse Park.

The park was a wide square of ground, inlaid with flower beds and footpaths and belted on four sides by wrought iron gating that resembled asparagus. The recent cold snap had stripped its trees of their leaves and discolored its grass, but it was still impressive. The dinner hour had reduced its usual hubbub of fashionable people to only a uniformed nanny pushing a baby carriage and an elderly couple who sat on a bench surrounded by bobbing pigeons.

"Watch me!" said Joe, as he parked the skato by the open front gate. He peeled off his shoes and socks and tore across the lawn. "Don't be a chicken! C'mon!"

Hannah glanced around. Nobody seemed to care what Joe was doing. Nor was anyone watching to see if Hannah would copy him. Discreetly, she unlaced and pulled off a shoe and stocking. Then their mates. It had been over a month, she realized, since she had been barefoot outdoors. She shrieked to feel the cold grass scratch the bottoms of her feet.

Joe shot the length of the park and was steering toward one of its largest willow trees. She saw him grip its lowest branch expertly, twisting himself up the trunk, then hauling his body still higher. Up and up. Was he allowed? She doubted it.

"Betcha can't climb a tree anymore, milkmaid!" Joe shouted.

She was already to the willow's base. "Betcha you're wrong!"

This tree was not as thick as Bloom, but its branches were lower and more plentiful. Hannah gripped and pulled herself until she was a full head higher than Joe. No, she had not forgotten a thing about trees.

Settled, she swung her feet, enjoying the bite of October cold on her toetips.

"Go careful," Joe warned, looking up at her. "This tree is trickier that it looks. I fell out of it a few months back. Bruise on my keister looked like I'd skid across a patch of motor oil."

"I'm safe," she assured him.

They stared across the cityscape. At the edge of the park's gate, the lamplighter propped his ladder, and soon the first light of a city evening sparked to a glow.

Hannah leaned back and threw her arms wide and up so that they brushed the feathery fringed tips of what few leaves remained. "This was a best day," she declared. "Thanks, Joe."

"Yeah, yeah, it was nothing."

"It was better than nothing."

"One thing about a city, there's always enough to do to push you out of a sulk," said Joe. "Even without me to show the way. And don't forget, when it comes to the competition, it's still you against me."

"You against me!" Hannah agreed.

22

BABY FACE NELSON

SUNDAY, JOE ignored Hannah. He galloped upstairs after she came home from church in the morning. He sneaked out of the house without her in the afternoon.

Perhaps he hadn't had any fun yesterday? Hannah slumped in the parlor's front window seat. Perhaps he preferred to be left alone?

A noise in the doorway startled her. She turned. Joe must have come inside through the kitchen. A worn brown notebook was tucked under his arm.

"Here's the thing," he said. "If you don't

know all there is to know about Baby Face
Nelson, I don't see how we're gonna be buddies.
You might say I'm off my head, but I feel like
he's a personal acquaintance of mine. You got
anyone like that?"

"Madame Curie and Pythagoras and Mae
West," Hannah answered.

"There you have it! And look here. Francis's
ma bakes on Sundays. Reading and eating, see,
they go together." Joe jumped up onto the window seat beside her, removed his cap, and pulled
a handkerchief-wrapped slice of butter cake
from his pocket. "We'll split."

Hannah broke the cake in half as Joe opened
his scrapbook across their laps. She stared at the
newsprint, a sly jumble of words set alongside
grainy photographs of storefronts or automobiles
or a close-up image of a man whose boneless face
appeared to have taken a few punches. "Mushy
Face Nelson, they ought to call him," she pronounced. "Oh, boy, the newsprint is too small!"

"Don't sulk. Reading's a cinch if you're on to

the right story," Joe answered. In one crocodile bite, he dropped a piece of cake into his mouth. Crumbs flew everywhere. "We'll begin at the beginning, how 'bout? First, I'll take you through the history on the official FBI report. You watch my finger hit the words." He brushed the crumbs off the page, cleared his throat, and began to speak in his "Ulysses" voice. "'Baby Face Nelson was born Lester M. Gillis in December 1908, in Chicago. He spent his youth roaming the city streets with his gang of juvenile hoodlums, committing petty crimes. By the age of fourteen, Baby Face was an accomplished car thief.'"

Hannah watched the words under Joe's finger as she listened to a story that was as good—if not better—than any radio program she'd ever heard. Baby Face was just a few years older than Hepp, and what a life he'd led! All that shoplifting, car stealing, street fighting, liquor smuggling, and bank robbing!

Joe had arranged the articles in sequence so that Baby Face's records read like a mystery thriller. He broke apart the harder words into chewable pieces.

Tom-my-gun. Fed-er-al in-ves-ti-ga-tion. Plain-clothes-men.

The light thinned as they wound their way through Baby Face's grisly history.

"Gosh, Joe," Hannah said, closing the book with a contented sigh after they had finished. "I do believe that is the best story I ever read."

"Toldja!" Joe grinned. Then he explained that with John Dillinger dead, Baby Face was now the FBI's Most Wanted. "Armed and dangerous!" Joe wriggled his eyebrows.

"How do you know Baby Face won't come to Philadelphia next?" squeaked Hannah.

"Uh-uh, he won't come here. Too many men in blue."

"But what about the banks?" Hannah insisted. "There's loads of banks in Philadelphia."

"Naw, see, you don't understand Baby Face. He's best in the heartland, where he can lay low from prying—"

"Aha! Joe and Hannah!" Neither of them had heard Mrs. Sweet enter the house. Startled, Hannah looked up to see her leaning slantways into the room. Her features were unpleasantly bunched, as if tied and held to the middle of her face by invisible string. "I'm looking for Beverly. Where is she?" She glanced at the empty piano bench as if Beverly ought to be there.

"She's out," said Joe. That Beverly spent her Sunday evenings with her regular beau, Charlie, was a secret from Mrs. Sweet.

"When she gets in, tell her that I want a word," said Mrs. Sweet. "No matter the time. Hear me? Tell her to knock on my door."

Hannah and Joe nodded. Mrs. Sweet turned and huffed upstairs.

"She didn't even say good night. D'you think something's wrong?" Hannah asked nervously.

"I don't know from wrong, but something's on the cooker," Joe answered.

23

ABANDONED

"YOU'RE GETTING the boot?" Joe's voice was incredulous.

Beverly nodded. "I've got two weeks' notice. Sweet tells me the new crop of students entering the Academy is too young and talented for me to compete. Classically trained," she whispered. She dabbed at her eyes. "Even if I passed the exams, I might not be guaranteed placement, and she doesn't want to chance it."

Hannah counted the chimes as the grandfather clock in the foyer struck midnight. An

173

hour earlier, on Beverly's knock, both she and Joe had sneaked downstairs, where Beverly had heated a pan of milk and poured it into mugs sweetened with sugar. Now Beverly raised her mug as if in a toast. "Truth is, Sweet wants a real, sensible maid." She took a long sip. "Someone who actually remembers to dust."

"Christmas!" Joe sputtered. "It was never about the dust! Who ever heard of a maid with fingers too soft to scrub a floor or press a sheet? You're the worst dratted maid in all of Philadelphia, Bev. But you're a fine musician."

Under the table, Hannah's fingers tapped an anxious rhythm. Her stomach felt pulled as taffy. What else could Beverly do, if she couldn't play music?

"Sweet told me a house of young people had been amusing at first, but we were starting to crowd her," said Beverly. "'It's true I've been lonely now that both my boys have left me,' she says. 'But what if I want to see in Paris in the springtime?' she says. 'Why's it left to me to mind you three, to serve your every need? I've bit off more than I chew.'" Beverly shook her head in disbelief. "Boarding us kids—it's been nothing but a rich folks' fad, if you ask me. Same as those puffy goose-down jackets ladies took to wearing last year."

"I'll wager there's plenty other families who'd take you in." Joe thudded a fist into his palm. "A beezillion people living a stone's throw from the Academy who are nuts for music, and who've got a spare room, and who aren't blasted dopes." He didn't sound convinced.

"There's no such number as beezillion," said Hannah. She knew it was the wrong thing to blurt out, but no one remarked on it.

"My luck's burnt down to the wire," said Beverly tiredly. "Charlie teaches piano, so he's always in the big fancy houses, and he says the newest trend is to bring poor students over from Europe to teach arts on the cheap."

"If Charlie teaches piano, maybe you could, too," Hannah suggested.

"Oh, sure I could, but that's no way to make a living." Beverly sighed. "Charlie's real paycheck comes from working down at the wharf. Piano's his hobby. Hannah, please quit drumming your fingers under the table. It's driving me bats." Beverly stood and pushed in her chair. "I don't have money to live on my own *and* work *and* study. I'll be eighteen next month. Too old for dreams."

"It's not fair," said Hannah. "It's not fair for Mrs. Sweet to close a door on you all of a sudden like that!"

Beverly shrugged, but her smile was sad. "Perhaps things'll look smoother by morning. I'll go to sleep and see. Good night, you two." She leaned over and dropped a kiss on each of their heads before slipping off through the kitchen door to her bedroom.

"Poor Bev," Hannah murmured. "Poor us, too. What if Mrs. Sweet wants to chuck us all out? What if it's true, Joe, that we're nothing but a fad?"

"Time will tell. But without Beverly around pretending to take care of things, this joint is gonna get pretty empty." Joe's voice was matter-of-fact to disguise the hurt in his face. More than once Joe had mentioned to Hannah that Beverly was the same age as his sister, Sally. In the short time they'd lived here, Beverly had become a big sister to them both. The house wouldn't be the same without Beverly and her music, thought Hannah miserably.

Apparently, however, Mrs. Sweet did not hear it that way.

PART THREE

24

A PHONE CALL

BEVERLY HAD packed and left by the end of the following week. Her "jiffy" plan, as she called it, was to lodge with Charlie's sisters until she got her bearings. After that, Beverly said, the future might land her anywhere.

"Anywhere there's a piano, you mean?" Hannah asked that last afternoon as she flopped herself upon the stripped mattress in Beverly's empty room. She felt as if she had asked the same question a hundred times before, but she could not bear to think of Beverly existing any-place without a piano.

"Stop fretting about me." Beverly already sounded more adult than she had a week ago. "Oh, and I've got a farewell gift for you, Hannah. I've been meaning to pass it along." She straightened and clasped her hands behind her back, professor-style. "It's on my authority that during his life, Ludwig van Beethoven wrote a total of thirty-two sonatas. Not only that, but Johannes Bach's thirty-two Goldberg Variations are among the best known of his works. How about that for your lucky number, thirty-two?"

"Gosh, sometimes thirty-two seems more than lucky," said Hannah wonderingly, "and closer to magical. Thanks, Bev."

"Oh, but that's not my gift," said Beverly. "This is—I stole some sheet music from the Academy. If you help me push my trunk out to the front hall for Charlie to pick up, I'll play you Bach's Aria and his first two Variations. What do you say?"

Hannah was already dragging the trunk by its

handles. "I'd say I'm all ears! This'll be the first concert you've ever played for me, Beverly."

"Guess I never had the time to spare, before."

Once the luggage was stacked at the front door, Hannah ran into the parlor and sat cross-legged on the ottoman. Beverly took her usual place behind the piano.

"Good-bye, Steinway, dear," she said softly, rubbing the piano's polished ebony surface. Then she spread her fingers over the keyboard and began.

Hannah closed her eyes as the short elegant stacks of sound marched and melted through her head. Beverly's mind must be full of counting patterns, too, Hannah thought. Except that Beverly's patterns made a tune instead of a proof or equation.

When Beverly finished, Hannah clapped and whistled through her teeth the way Joe had taught her. "Oh, Bev, I'm sure going to miss you. Who'll sing along to Bing Crosby with me now?"

"Joe might, for a nickel." The corner of Beverly's mouth tucked up, the first smile Hannah had seen from her all day.

Even after Charlie rang the doorbell and Beverly was gone, Hannah could hear the echo of her music. Once the sound of the piano playing had given Hannah pangs of homesickness. Now, in the silence, Hannah missed Beverly instead.

Before she left, Beverly had roasted a chicken and boiled some potatoes and parsnips for Hannah and Joe's supper, but the next evening, with the kitchen dark and Mrs. Sweet nowhere in sight, there was another downside to Beverly's absence. Hannah prepared no-fuss horseradish-and-ham sandwiches while Joe chopped a tomato salad.

Midway through their meal, Joe lifted his head. "Sweet's back."

Hannah strained to listen. "She sneaks in so quiet, you'd need the ears of a bat to hear her."

"She doesn't want us to hear, otherwise she'd hafta stop in for a chat." Joe rolled his eyes.

"Even if we both the pass the exam, we'll need another house to hang our hats come June," he warned. "Mark my words."

Now Hannah could detect a ghostlike footstep in the upstairs hall.

"Say, it's Thanksgiving next week," Joe remarked. "Are you spending it with friends?"

"Oh, no. I've got too much work."

"Me, either," said Joe with a wink. "Snobs."

"Snobs," she agreed.

From the hall, the telephone jangled. Neither of them looked in its direction. The telephone was always for Mrs. Sweet, and so it was all the more surprising when her voice resounded through the air vent.

"Haaa-naaah," she called. "You're wanted on the telephone!"

Joe raised his eyebrows.

Hannah's heart jounced. She jumped up and ran out of the kitchen to the hall phone and she picked up the heavy receiver. "Yes? Who is there?"

"Hannah!" Ma's voice sounded small but close, almost as if she were in the next room.

"Ma! Is something wrong? Why are you at the Applebees'?"

"No, I'm right here in the kitchen. Pa and I decided to install a telephone."

"Oh!" Hannah tried to picture her mother speaking into a telephone mouthpiece. It seemed too movie star-ish for Ma.

"Folks change their milk orders last minute," Ma explained, "and with you and Hepp gone, we ought to be in touch. You simply tell the operator to connect you to Chadds Ford, Bennett, number seventy-two."

"Seventy-two," Hannah repeated. The number of inches in six feet. The number of days it took Nellie Bly to travel the world. Now, the telephone number. The future had poked in its nose and turned into the present.

Over the line, Ma was skittering on in a breathless manner about how the telephone man had come to install the line and had run the cord wrong, before she abruptly interrupted herself. "But that's not what I rang you up for, Hannah. I'm not sure how to say this without being able to see you, but I suppose there's no other way." Ma's breath on the line was as loud as radio static.

"What is it, Ma?"

"The reason I called was to say that. To say that. That Pa and I hoped you might be able to free yourself to come home for a spell. Tomorrow."

"Is something the matter, Ma? Is the family well? Is there word from Hepp?"

"Mrs. Bennett, Miss Bennett," interrupted the switchboard operator. "You'll have to get off the line. There's a few callers wanting to get hold of Mrs. Sweet."

"Another moment, thank you," said Ma. "Hannah, it's your grandfather."

"What's news of Granddad?" asked Hannah. Her fingers twisted the phone cord to keep herself from tapping. "Is he in trouble? Is he hurt?"

"Hannah, Granddad McNaughton passed

away last night. In his sleep, peacefully." Now Ma was speaking quickly, as if she were in a train moving faster and faster away from Hannah. "You'll need to hurry home for the funeral this Sunday. There's a train that leaves the city tomorrow morning at eight sharp. Pa will pick you up at the station. Please ask Mrs. Sweet if we might borrow expenses for the ticket and send the reimbursement back with you. I'm sorry to give you this news. Hurry home, Hannah!"

The line clicked as Ma hung up. Hannah was left staring into the receiver. Her mind whirled, though her feet seemed to be made of clay. No, no, it couldn't be, she thought wildly. Impossible. Last night, when? Last night, when she was studying Mr. Cole's worksheet about capacity in customary units? Or when she had been brushing her teeth, or arguing with Joe about who was the better baseball player, Dizzy Dean or his brother Daffy?

Surely some part of her ought to have felt it—a confused, drowning rush of grief that she could mark in her head as the same moment her grandfather had departed.

But last night had been so ordinary!

The nagging voice of the operator finally pushed Hannah from her trance, reminding her that Mrs. Sweet's call was being connected, and that she had better run and fetch her.

25

HOME AGAIN

PA KEPT HIS eyes on the road as the truck rattled and looped along the familiar route. He had been the first person whom Hannah had spied when the train pulled in. Standing alone in his denim coveralls and brown field coat, he was instantly recognizable, and yet it seemed an eternity since Hannah had seen him last.

She had been scared that Pa would look older, or different, but he did not. In fact, it was she who seemed to take him aback.

"Sakes, you're a sight, Hannah," he said,

reaching out to tug the snipped ends of her hair, then stepping back to look her up and down. "Nothing but sunk eyes and bony legs. Don't they feed you in Philadelphia?"

She shook her head. "There's too much on the table, if anything."

Pa's forehead wrinkled, but he did not respond.

They climbed into the truck and fell into silence. Hannah could not pluck up the nerve to ask any questions about Granddad. Pa and Granddad had shared a cantankerous relation-ship, further strained by the fact that Pa worked a property Granddad had partly and stubbornly owned. In her parents' hearts, Hannah realized, Granddad's passing must have come qualified with slight relief.

"Will Hepp show for the funeral?" she asked instead.

"Dunno. We sent word by telegram to Kansas City day before last, but heard nothing back. He must have cleared out beforehand."

Hannah caught the note of Pa's irritation.

It had never made sense to Pa that Hepp could drift in and out of touch with the family so easily.

She stared out the window. Chadds Ford was dressed for winter. Cooled of color, stripped of blossom, with the sinking sun pulling the last bit of haze from the sky, it was not the prettiest time of season. Yet the familiarity of it set a lump in her throat.

A midday dinner was ready when she and Pa walked through the kitchen door. Over the steaming pot roast, Ma appeared tired, but Roy whooped and squeezed Hannah, jumping her up and down until she thought she'd crack a lung. These months as an only child must have been lonesome for Roy, she figured.

"Jeepers-creepers! You went and chopped your best feature into a haystack." Roy tousled her hair once he released her. "And you look worn through."

"Hannah, you've been studying too hard," reprimanded Ma.

"No, I haven't." Her family's concern baffled her. Pleased her, too. It was nice to be fussed over.

During the meal, Ma heaped Hannah's plate and kept an eye that she ate everything on it, and Roy even leaped up to fetch a glass of milk, while Pa made remarks about the dangerous effects of polluted city air. With all the attention foisted on her, it was not until the end of the meal that Hannah noticed.

"But where's Ben?"

"He left a week ago. Day after he collected his paycheck," said Pa.

"Nobody even saw him leave," Roy added. "He must have hopped a midnight train back to Ohio. Caught us all by surprise. Suppose he'd had enough of being away, and needed to get back home." Roy hesitated, then said, "We kept thinking you'd do the same, Han."

"Me?" It had never crossed her mind to leave the city as long as Granddad kept watch over her progress there. After all, it was to him that she had sent her graded math tests and Mr. Cole's weekly evaluation reports.

Granddad was the reason I left Chadds Ford, thought Hannah as she helped Ma tidy the kitchen afterward. Now Granddad has left Chadds Ford, too. Where does that put me? The question circled, searching for an answer that lay outside her reach.

Entering her bedroom later that evening was like reuniting with a childhood friend. Hannah tapped its corners and straightened and reordered her personal items; her faded, half-forgotten collection of Rudy Vallee press clippings, her stuffed calico horse. Though the night was too cold for it, she cracked open her window so that she could listen to the round echo of owl song.

She changed into her nightgown and climbed into bed, relishing its familiar softness. She imagined Granddad sitting on his porch, impeccably dressed, alone but never lonely. Her eyes would not close as she whispered problems for him to solve.

"If Granddad McNaughton smokes eight cigarettes and eats three fifteen-ounce servings of watermelon at four pennies an ounce . . . "

She fell asleep with images of Granddad in her head and an ache in her heart.

The next morning, Ma had to knock twice on Hannah's door to rouse her for chores. She felt as if she were moving through glue. Throughout the milking and breakfast, she tried to smother her sadness, but more than once she caught Roy peering intently at her.

As they walked together ahead of Ma and Pa the half mile to the church, Roy threw an arm around her shoulders. "Lean in, if you'd like," he said. "Poor sis. You're a walking advertisement for why I'd never live in a city."

The church was airless and crowded with familiar faces. Tru and Betsy burst from their pews to hug her, whispering promises to visit as soon as they could get away. It seemed as if the whole of Chadds Ford had come to pay respects to Granddad. As many people as could fill a

Saturday matinee in Philadelphia, Hannah realized. The main difference being that she could
recite every name in this entire congregation.

So many kind smiles, so much concern as
folks stopped by the Bennett pew to pass along a
consoling word about Dr. McNaughton. The
Arnolds, the Applebees, the Dilworths, the
Winnickers, the Seals. Even Miss Cascade was
present, wearing a new pair of spectacles,
Wendell Nutley at her elbow. The closeness of
Chadds Ford struck Hannah solemn and real as
a church bell, holding her to all she had left
behind.

As Mrs. Lind struck up the organ, Hannah
inclined slightly into Ma's side. In other days,
when she and Granddad had found themselves in
the midst of crowds, they had invented percentage
problems. Now Hannah tried to pick up the thread
of the game. What percentage of people wore
stripes, how many had mustaches, how many carried hymnals in their left hands versus right?
Questions washed in and answers washed out.

Reverend Kenyon's voice rumbled from the pulpit as he spoke of Granddad, building up his smarts to make up for his general grouchiness. The memory of summertime on Granddad's porch spread upward from Hannah's feet, and her eyelids grew heavy as she imagined herself and Granddad sitting together, making wishes on watermelon seeds.

"Hannah!" Ma hissed. "Hannah, wake up!"

Hannah's eyes snapped open as she caught her breath. Faces were turned toward her. What had she done?

Reverend Kenyon was not speaking. He frowned down at Hannah and roughly cleared his throat.

Roy leaned forward past Ma. "Sis! You were snoring!" he whispered.

No! So disrespectful! How could she have done such a thing? Now Hannah sensed the amusement in the room, the collective smile that Hannah Bennett might have gone off to Philadelphia to fill her mind with math, but she was the same unpolished, unfinished Hannah as ever.

Blushing, Hannah folded her hands and looked down at her lap, but she pinched the tops of her legs so that she would stay awake for the rest of the service. At least there were no Ottley girls present to poke fun.

Reverend Kenyon cleared his throat once more and resumed.

26

HEPP

HANNAH MATCHED her mother's long strides as they made their way home. Pa and Roy had stayed behind with some of the other men to help with the burial, and most of the congregation would be stopping by the house later for refreshments.

"Well, it's done, then," said Ma. "Your granddad's in heaven now, pestering the angels. Oh, I'll miss him, though. He'd been failing a while, but naturally he refused to see a specialist. Doctors make terrible patients." She shook her head, rueful. "He wouldn't give up his smoking nor his chew, even with that cough. Said the tobacco refreshed his lungs, though I'm sure the effect was directly opposite."

Hannah agreed with a nod.

"There's things at the house Granddad wanted you to have. Books and such," said Ma. "You'll need to sort through."

Hannah nodded again. She listened to the crunch of their boots on the frost-hardened earth.

When Ma spoke once more, it was as if the words had been mulling inside her. "You ought to know, Hannah, we've sold Granddad's property to the Winnickers."

This time, Hannah could not be silent. "Why, how awful!" she blurted. "Elgin Winnicker living in Granddad's house? But Elgin's such a blasted chump, he can hardly tell the difference between a numerator and a denominator!"

"Such language, Hannah!—and it can't be helped. We need the cash money," said Ma.

"We're going to use some of it to build on to the dairy. Pa is hiring extra labor, and we want to buy a pasteurizer. Keep ourselves a step ahead." She paused, then hurried on. "Which means to say that a lot is happening here. And you might want to think about returning home to help Pa and Roy and me. Home for keeps." Ma's voice softened. "Where you belong, where you'll be healthy and watched over and lonely no more."

"I haven't been lonely," Hannah said stiffly. It was a struggle to lie to her mother. She had not mentioned her loneliness in any of her letters home. She did not want to confess to it now.

"Oh, Hannah, it's not hard to see that—"

"Ahoy, there! Ma! Hannah!"

At the sound of the voice, they both looked toward their house, which loomed on the horizon. Hannah could just make out the outline of a familiar figure standing on the front porch. At the same instant, they recognized him.

"Why, you!" exclaimed Ma under her breath. "You!"

Bunching their skirts, they sprinted the remaining distance. Ma, in a spurt of coltish energy, beat Hannah by a pace.

Hepp, at last! Hannah hugged him hard once Ma let him go. Immediately, she saw the changes in her oldest brother. He was thinner, the bones of his cheeks and shoulders and collarbone whittled sharp, his hands felt callused in her own, and he sported a fibrous mustache redder than the auburn of his hair.

"Just arrived. I had to walk from the station," he told them. His smile turned solemn. "There's not a body on the road. The whole town must be eulogizing. I'll pay my private respects to Granddad tomorrow."

"Some of the congregation will be by here later," said Ma. "So you can have a proper reunion with everyone in town."

There was a knock at the back door. "But that's awfully early for the guests," said Ma, startled. She went to answer it, and returned a moment later looking preoccupied. "A tramp outside wants dinner and shelter. I'll give him food, some milk, and he can stay overnight in the barn with a quilt and pillow."

As Hepp and Hannah watched, Ma shook some coins from her crockery pot on the windowsill. "And seven cents to see him on his way," she said, counting it out. "That'll have to do. I spent nearly every penny on a Thanksgiving turkey from Brandywine River Farm. Oh, it's a shame. Two days' time and there'd be meat to give him, along with pie and chestnut stuffing. He looks so gaunt, I'd like to send him off with more."

"But I have money!" Hannah cried as she ran to her coat that hung from the hall peg. She dug out her aluminum-collecting money, her two dimes and three pennies, and added it to the pile in her mother's hand. "Thirty cents," she pronounced. "That's a better number."

"Better," said Ma, and she hurried out to tend to the stranger.

27

THE HEART OF IT

HEPP HAD matured, everyone agreed. Although he had developed no more passion for the dairy, he was reliable with chores, and his storytelling kept the mealtime hour filled with intrigue. The return of Hepp's easy, lighthearted presence pulled everyone into a joyful mood.

Without quite intending to, Hannah swept thoughts of Mrs. Sweet and the Wexler Scholarship and Ottley Friends into a corner of her mind and left them there. She never shared stories of Philadelphia. Not that anyone pressed her. Nobody inquired of her studies. Nobody asked whether or not she would pass next month's exams.

Hannah reasoned that, with Hepp home, she would stay through Thanksgiving, but that day came and left without any talk of her returning to the city. By then, her hands had reacquainted themselves with her old chores so easily, it was as if she had never left them off. She was concerned, though, about the pending telephone call from Mrs. Sweet, and her mind tumbled with different excuses.

Only, Mrs. Sweet did not telephone.

Home Is Where the Heart Is promised the faded cross-stitch on a pillow Ma kept on the horsehair sofa in the front room. Hannah had aired out, plumped up, and propped her feet on that pillow countless times without pondering its meaning. Now the words pulled at her with new insistence.

Yet every night, opening her Level Seven math book, she seemed to turn into another self.

By lamplight, she reviewed her worksheets and drafted new ones. She even labeled them with Mr. Cole's whimsical headlines—*Geometry Chums! Keen Scalenes!* She could almost feel Mr. Cole's glass eye hovering over the house, brilliant and coolly watchful as the moon.

I must get back to Ottley Friends, Hannah insisted to herself. No matter how much I detest it there. I'm three math levels higher than any other girl in my grade. I can't be blown back, even if my heart is here at home. Granddad would have hated for me to quit.

And yet her convictions seemed to fade with each sunrise.

Saturday dawned. After that morning's milking, Pa, Hepp, Roy, and Hannah trooped into the kitchen to find coffee on the boil, eggs in the poacher, and sections of *The Chronicle* scattered on the table.

"You have the weekend paper delivered?" Hannah asked as she reached for it.

"It's Will Emery's new job," Ma told her.

"He's trying to make some money delivering *The Chronicle* and *The Little Bee* to the area."

"Rolls up here in his daddy's half-broke Hudson quarter past six on the dot," Pa added. "Noise to wake the dead."

"Oh, we're already awake, and it hardly costs," Ma said. "The neighbors are chipping in. The Emery farm is in danger of foreclosure this spring."

"Look at you, Hannah Bennett! Pretending to read the National news section with more airs than Mrs. Vanderbilt." Hepp reached across the table and batted the paper at its crease. Hannah shook it out indignantly.

"I can read *some* words," she retorted.

Roy grinned and watched from where he stood at the door, a biscuit in one hand as he used the other to button his overcoat. He was teaching himself to drive by taking over the morning milk deliveries. Bit by bit, Roy was learning how to manage the entire farm and dairy. He would be the one to run it one day. Hannah saw that now.

Hepp tweaked her ear. "What are these *some* words telling you?"

"For your information, I'm following an item on Baby Face Nelson," she said. "He's on the lam. Stole a car in Nevada and he's heading north toward the Corn Belt. But he'll never get caught. He's got coppers so spun around they'll need eyes in the back of their head to catch his tail."

"Listen to you!" Hepp snorted.

"How can you read about such horrors in the world?" asked Ma. "Hardened criminals like Mr. Nelson are who keep me up nights!"

"Ma, it takes nothing to keep you up nights." Hepp laughed. "Two years ago, you were locking our bedroom windows against baby kidnappers, and all of us full grown!"

"World is full of troubled and troublesome people, and it's your ma's right to lock a window against 'em," said Pa, raising a hand against Hepp's laughter and closing the subject.

Hepp went quiet but his glare trapped Pa's a moment too long. Last evening, Pa and Hepp had argued over the best way to repair some fencing out in the south pasture. It was the same tired back-and-forth, the same old struggle between them. Hannah suspected that it would not be long before Hepp itched to leave home and travel again.

The way life used to be was not the way it was meant to last.

28

PLEASE YOURSELF

LATER THAT DAY, Hannah pulled on her coat and walked to the cemetery in search of a solitary moment of prayer for Granddad.

Instead, she found Hepp sprawled flat on his stomach on a barn blanket. He was reading a book.

"Gee, it seems chilly for picnics, don't you think?"

Hepp looked up. "Last winter, I lived in a Hooverville outside Chicago. Since then, I learned I can read just about anywhere. Plus Granddad McNaughton feels close to me here. Wish there'd been time for one last visit—not that I was special to him, grumpy old man that he was." He shut the book. "But he would have liked this. John Muir, *Travels in Alaska.*" He rolled up to sit, leaning back on his elbows, as Hannah dropped down onto the blanket beside him. She touched Granddad's simple headstone that stood next to the marker for Grandma McNaughton, who had died before Hannah was born. Granddad's dates were 1866–1934.

"Thirty-four years in each century," she noted. "An even divide, just the way Granddad would have wanted." Then she leaned back against the slab and tried to grasp the cold, real fact of it. Her eyes filled.

"Say, when are ya heading back to Philly, city slicker?" Hepp's coaxing cowboy drawl made Hannah laugh even as she rubbed at her eyes.

"I'm no slicker." She nudged Hepp in the ribs with the toe of her boot.

"Ah, but the city's changed you," Hepp contended. "Question is, for the better?"

"Our folks don't think so. All I'm hearing is how pale and tired I look. But if I don't get back by next week, I ought not to return at all," said Hannah. "I'll be too far behind in my studies."

Hepp stretched out his legs, crossing his feet in their funny shoes that were made of a thin, clownish rubber that Hannah had never seen before. "Then why are you still knocking around?"

"Suppose I'm confused," Hannah answered honestly. The interest in Hepp's face encouraged her to continue. "It's likely I won't pass that blamed exam, and I'd been dreading my defeat in Granddad's eyes. He was so sure I'd be his legacy. Now he won't have to witness my failure."

Hepp ran a thoughtful finger over his new mustache. "Pass or fail, you'd disappoint Granddad's memory if you copped out altogether," he said. "To quit now might not sit easy with you, either."

Hannah nodded. She knew it was true, but it was still hard to hear. "How do you do it, Hepp?" she asked. "With all your traveling.

How do you step into a new place and make it yours?"

"It's not against the rules to slip a bit of your old home into the new. You're only as much a stranger as you want to be. Simple, really." Hepp stood. "I'll leave you to your time alone. Gotta keep moving, anyhow, so Pa can't catch me reading." Briefly, he rested a hand on the crown of Hannah's head. "Granddad's passing must be hard on you. But I suppose it was burdensome, too. He was tough to please. Now you're free to please yourself. Remember to bring in that blanket."

Hepp set off down the hill. He had lost his childlike lope, Hannah noticed, but he had gained a stance that would not tip over easy.

"He *was* hard to please," she said softly to herself. "But when he was pleased, there was nobody happier." And she knew that some part of her would continue trying to please Granddad. Even if he was no longer here in the space of his body, she would always feel connected to the space of his soul.

29

NOBODY'S SWEETHEART

TRU AND BETSY came to visit late that afternoon. Tru had brought half a mince pie and Betsy, her ridge-grip jump rope.

Three were not enough jumpers for a real team, and it was too cold and getting dark, besides, but Hannah shooed Homer and the hens out of the way so that the girls could set up a game in the side yard. Tru had invented a count from a new radio song.

Who's that little chatter-box?
The one with curl-ee auburn locks?
Who do you see?

It's Lit-tle Or-phan An-nee!
Count all the orphans,
How many do you see?
One, two, three, four, five, six, seven . . .

Hannah counted to only fourteen orphans before she tangled and tripped. Then she and Tru turned the rope and watched as Betsy, braids flopping, jumped and jumped until Hannah's hand began to hurt.

"You've gotten expert!" Hannah exclaimed.

"And you're out of practice!" Betsy retorted. "Don't you have any good jump-rope partners in the city?"

Hannah shrugged and let the question go unanswered.

Afterward, the threesome gathered in the kitchen for Tru's pie along with hot cider spiked with cinnamon sticks. The girls told Hannah all of the gossip about school and sweethearts. Elgin was sweet on Melinda and had given her a sandalwood jewelry box that opened to play

"The Great Crooner"—which by now they were all sick to death of hearing. Tru still preferred Hollywood men to Chadds Ford boys, and was sweeter on Clark Gable than Lane Chandler these days. Betsy was sweet on Roy—but a hawkish look from Betsy stopped that piece of news midway out of Tru's mouth.

And did Hannah have a sweetheart? Their eyes were shiny, waiting.

Hannah pressed her mug to her lips and held back her answer, though she was thinking of Joe. He was different from her sweetheart, she realized. Joe Elway just might be her best friend, same as Tru and Betsy were each other's best friends. But how could she explain to them that a boy was her best friend? How would they hear it without twisting her arm for another meaning?

"No," Hannah answered after a lingering moment. "My school is only girls. Fact is, I hardly know any boys these days."

"How wretched!" exclaimed Betsy. "Poor you. That sure takes the fun out. And the girls?"

"Hateful," said Hannah. "Full of airs and snubs."

"Why, I could have told you that, silly!" said Tru, a lilt of satisfaction in her voice. "What did you expect? Oh, Hannah, stay here next week for the church tea dance! Everyone'll be there, and you could use some real fun."

"Besides, if you're not meeting any fellas, how'll we all become June brides?" demanded Betsy. "And live down the street from each other in our own dear little white houses? Mine with green shutters and Tru's with red shutters and yours with blue shutters!"

Hannah had forgotten about her white house with its blue shutters. She missed chatting with the girls, too, and jumping rope, and hearing the school gossip. She missed all of it dearly. But her mind's eye could not seem to picture herself in that white and blue house. Perhaps it was because she did not have a sweetheart.

Later that evening, up in her room, Hannah sat at her desk and picked up her math book. She fanned its pages. She had finished the workbook exercises the night before, and her Level Seven book was complete. If she wanted a challenge, she would have to get hold of Level Eight, which was propped on Mr. Cole's crowded shelf. If Mr. Cole sent the book to Chadds Ford by post, she could teach herself. But Level Nine was an introduction to calculus, a fresh learning expedition that demanded the expert guidance of Mr. Cole.

If she stayed in Chadds Ford, the mysteries of Level Nine and every level thereafter would remain unanswered.

Abruptly, Hannah stood and paced her room thirty-two times. She stopped and looked out her window at the moon. It wasn't fair. She itched to know. She craved to know, or Levels Nine and Ten and onward and upward would tempt and haunt her forever.

Perhaps there was no one correct place to be. Whatever she decided, she would be acting on instinct. And that would have to be reason enough.

30

WOODEN KIMONO

BY EARLY NEXT morning, Hannah was packed and ready to go.

"My mind's made up," she stated during breakfast after the milking. "I thought Roy might drop me off for the early train while he made his delivery rounds."

She knew from their faces that Ma and Pa were unhappy to receive this news. Roy went stubbornly mute. Hannah could feel her mouth fix in a determined line. She looked to her older brother for help.

"Good girl," said Hepp, firmly on Hannah's side. "About time."

There was a silence. Then Pa set down his fork. "No Bennetts are quitters, anyhow," he said. "Take that dollar from my wallet. It's in my jacket hanging on the peg. Ought to pay your way, plus you owe some to Mrs. Sweet." He looked at Ma.

"Suppose you owe Mrs. Sweet the effort, as well," agreed Ma slowly, adding, "and completing that exam would have been your grandfather's wish. Let me make you a lunch. I believe there's a tin of sardines in the pantry, and some Thanksgiving turkey to take along."

It was decided. No one would hold her back, neither by guilt nor doubts nor reason. Hannah held tight to her emotions as she made her good-byes. Luckily, Hepp would be staying on in Chadds Ford through the week, which softened the blow, for Ma especially.

Hepp's hug ended in a slight push of Hannah's shoulders toward the door.

Silent, Roy carried Hannah's bags and flung them into the cab. He drove the truck too fast, too, with gripped fists and a marksman's concentration on the road. "But will you continue on, Hannah, even if you do make the grade?" he asked finally, breaking his own silence as the Chadds Ford train station came into sight. "How would you expect to spend *years* away from home?" His voice cracked on its edge.

Years was hard for Hannah to think about, too. She felt dizzy, but she tried to attribute it to Roy's perilous driving.

"I'd rather you wish me luck than leave me worries," she said. "Pass or fail, I'll be home for Christmas."

"Good luck, then," said Roy, "for what it's worth. I'll double back here when I'm done my deliveries, to see that the train got you. Or if you changed your mind."

As Hannah watched the truck drive away, old fears gripped her. She imagined herself calling Roy back, skipping and chasing behind the truck like a tumbleweed. What a peaceful morning it would be if she could share it with her brother, delivering milk to their neighbors.

Even the engine's whistle sounded lonely when the train eventually pulled in.

The force of her step hid the quaver of her spirit as Hannah boarded. She found a seat on the aisle so that she did not have to watch the countryside pass by. Instead, she flipped back through her Level Seven book. "Level Eight will be in my hands by tomorrow," she reminded herself in a whisper. She ate her cheese-and-sardine sandwich without looking to see whose nose she offended.

Entering Suburban Station, Hannah ran into the headline everywhere, both in bold black newspaper type as well as in the urgent echoing chants of the newsboys.

BABY FACE NELSON SHOT DEAD!

BODY FOUND IN CEMETERY DITCH!

She fished a discarded *Philadelphia Inquirer* from one of the dustbins and stood frozen in place, trying to make sense of the news.

Poor Joe!

She picked through the words. Baby Face had not stood a chance. Special Agent Hoover wasn't as thick as Joe had said. But Hoover's right-hand men, Cowley and Hollis, both had been killed in the line of duty. It was a terrible shame. Two good lives dashed out in the name of one scoundrel. Hannah had never warmed to Baby Face. She was frankly relieved that he had met his bloody end.

She rolled the paper under her arm to finish the article on the subway, where she became so engrossed that she missed her stop and had to haul her bags down five city blocks in the freezing cold. Strangers grumbled and stepped around her.

"'Scuse me! Coming through!" She whistled in her best imitation of Joe.

It was not raining, but the afternoon was dark and soggy, nearly the same weather as that first day Hannah had arrived, only now with a winter bite. The sky was lumpy as a bowl of mush. As

she walked past Rittenhouse Square Park,
Hannah saluted her willow. A familiar tree was
better than no familiar living thing at all.

She arrived at 5 Delancey Place to find it
quiet. She spied Joe through the open door of his
bedroom, his boots on and facedown on his bed.
When she crept closer and spoke his name, he
turned his head, and she saw that his eyes were
red-rimmed.

She perched on the edge of the bed. "Gosh,
Joe, I'm real sorry about Baby Face. I know he
meant a lot to you. A terrible end."

"Did you read he took seventeen bullets?" Joe
turned his baleful eyes on her. "I never thought
that fella'd get the wooden kimono. Nope, I never
thought it for a minute, milkmaid."

Milkmaid. Joe had not used that nickname in
a while.

"Perhaps it was his time," she said.

"Christmas! The good guys never win," Joe
lamented. "Ever!"

It did not seem to Hannah that Baby Face

Nelson could have so much as breathed the same air as the good guys. Some people's heroes were beyond comprehension.

"Are you hungry? My ma packed me some leftovers." Hannah jumped up. "I'll warm them on the stovetop for us, and we'll have a feast."

"Sounds fine. Thought I'd seen the last of you," Joe admitted. "The headmistress of Ottley Friends, that Miss Jordan, has been ringing up here every second. I musta took down a gadzillion messages on the phone pad. If Sweet weren't up in Boston, she'd likely boot you for missing more school than you said. Crumple up the notes, and she'll never be the wiser. And don't tell me there's no such number as gadzillion."

"All right, I won't," said Hannah, "even if there isn't."

In the kitchen, Hannah found the red wax pencil Beverly had used to make grocery lists. She opened the back door and on it drew a perfect X. Maybe tramps did not come to 5

Delancey Place, but there was plenty of food in this house. Now any passerby could see it plainly. It was one piece of Hepp's advice she could put into effect. She would add some of her old home into the new. Starting with hospitality.

FUTURE PERFECT

UPON HER RETURN from Boston, Mrs. Sweet summoned Hannah and Joe to the parlor, where she give them the news they had been waiting for. "The Wexler scholarship exams will be held at Thomas Jefferson High School in North Philadelphia on December eighteenth," she announced. "It's rumored that nearly one hundred students have registered.

"My bridge partner, Rose DeVrees, has a boarder, a scrap of a thing from Providence, Rhode Island, who received full academic aid on a Carnegie Scholarship. But I told Rose that our Hannah could count numbers from here to Timbuktu." The hungry smile Hannah knew well by now appeared in Mrs. Sweet's face. "Oh, I can pick a clever child from the herd. I wasn't appointed to the Mayor's Education Reform Board for nothing. Run along, now. I expect you've both got plenty of studying to do."

The test was twenty days away, Hannah noted when she was back in her bedroom. Twenty. She tried to get a feel for the number. Twenty was where calcium appeared in the Periodic Chart. 20/20 was perfect vision. Yes, Hannah reassured herself. Twenty meant strong bones and sharp eyes and good luck.

"Miss Jordan says I deserve a scholarship," Hannah told Joe the next night after supper. "But, Joe, if each teacher says that to each student, then which ones of us don't deserve it?"

"*I* deserve it," said Joe. "I'm smart and I'm ready." He knotted a length of butcher's twine tight around the remains of a beef brisket while

Hannah held the paper in place. They had taken to packing their leftovers into a hamper for Mr. Barnaby, who had come to Hannah's aid when she had inquired about local soup kitchens. Mr. Barnaby's fiancée, Eleanor, said she could use anything for the Goodwill with much appreciation.

Hannah wished she had thought of it beforehand. Sometimes the simplest learning came so slow.

"Do you think I deserve it?" she asked. "Honest, Joe. Do you think I'm ready?"

"Who knows? You against me, remember? But it's a crying shame to give out a taste of learning and then egg-candle us, looking for our dark spots. Picking out the best, sending home the rest." Joe began to jump around the kitchen, tossing the wrapped brisket and catching it like a football.

Joe was a piece of India rubber these days, Hannah decided. With the exams approaching, he bounced harder and higher. He was reaching to grab the scholarship with both hands.

I'm reaching high, too, Hannah thought. I deserve it as much as Joe, don't I?

She could not imagine working any harder, and yet at the same time she could feel herself sinking deeper into the usual obstructions. Patterns and sequences began to crowd in thickly from their safe edges to the center of her day. Thirty-two absorbed more time than usual. Sixteen wipes of each side of her face with her washcloth, sixteen raps upon each side of a plate before eating from it, sixteen chews on either side of her mouth before swallowing. She even paced thirty-two times around her room every time she entered or left. It made her comings and goings cumbersome.

Thirty-two did not stop at the door of Ottley Friends, either. Hannah found herself tapping any doorknob thirty-two taps before using it. Thirty-two was how many times the point of her pencil had to touch the upper right-hand corner of her paper before she got to work.

The girls noticed. They giggled or made fun, but one of them must have complained to Miss

Jordan. When Miss Jordan summoned Hannah to her office, she was sympathetic.

"I'll tell you a secret, Hannah. I always triple-check the locks on my front door before I go to sleep." Miss Jordan leaned forward. "Not once, not twice, but three times!" She laughed gently. Her face was open, inviting Hannah's confidence. "To me, triple-checking is a safeguard against danger. Is that what you believe your tapping and counting might be? A safeguard against dangers?"

"It was Helene Lyon who ratted me out, wasn't it?"

"Hannah, what an expression! And that's not the point. The point is that you must try to stop these impulses."

"I'll try to hide them better, Miss Jordan," Hannah answered truthfully, "but I don't think I can stop." Even as she spoke, her fingers itched to tap a pattern on her knees. Her heart was beating fast and frustration prickled at her skin.

"Dear, there's no need to shout." Miss Jordan held out her empty hands, palms up. "I wish

I comprehended your affliction, Hannah. It couldn't be easy for you. But you've come so far. It would a shame if you stumbled on account of this distress."

Hannah nodded and blinked first one eye then the other.

Onetwothreefour. Onetwothreefour.

And again. And again.

"You are driving yourself into a state," observed Miss Jordan. "You need to relax and take deep breaths. Also remember to chew your food slowly, and get plenty of sleep."

Hannah could feel her cheeks and temper flame. As if she didn't know that! As if she wanted patterns of thirty-two galloping around and around her brain like tireless horses on a racetrack! Miss Jordan talked as if tapping might be cured with the right trick, like having someone scare you to stop your hiccups!

Thank goodness for Joe, the one chum who had made the world shrink to a comfortable size. During their evenings of supper and study at the kitchen table, Joe's good-natured conversation provided freedom from the grip of her day.

"These word problems are dopey," Joe declared one night, looking up from a set of drills that Hannah had created just for him. "Christmas! Who cares how many cakes of soap Mr. Hooper sells, or how many miles Milo walks in five point three hours? I say, take the bus, Milo!"

"Math always means something. It always has an answer. I'll tell you what's dopey—grammar." Hannah scowled at her primer. "These tenses—ugh! The past progressive. The future perfect. 'I will have been gone.' 'We will have been finished.' Why is it called the future perfect? It's neither."

"The future perfect," said Joe patiently, "is easy as fish stew."

"You're cracked!" Hannah threw her arms open wide. "The future perfect is like saying that what *had* happened and what *will* happen have crashed into each other, like trains on the same rail out of different stations!"

"Well, all right." Joe laughed. "Read something good, instead. Look here, I've saved you a clipping on our boy Dutch Schultz. He's out on parole for tax fraud in New York, but if I know the Dutchman, he'll get himself off scot-free."

Joe drew a square of folded newspaper from his trouser pocket and flipped it across the table. "Go on, read it. Schultz is Hoover's plus Mayor LaGuardia's new Public Enemy Number One. I'm starting a new scrapbook on him. All right, don't read it, then. Gee, you're so het up, lately, Hannah."

"I am not!"

"You are, too."

"Am not!"

"Are, too, and you should see your face!" Joe looked around, then pushed up from his chair and crossed the kitchen, where he detached the silver metal teakettle from its hook above the sink. He brought it back and held it in front of Hannah as if it were a mirror. "Look!"

Hannah stared at her dented, lopsided image.

She was no Joan Crawford, no Claudette Colbert, either, but her fierce eyes and the passion of feeling that ignited her face startled her so much that she burst out laughing.

"Well, if I'm het up, then so are you," she retorted. "Only you bounce, while I boil."

"I won't argue with that," Joe admitted. "And I won't argue with you. But you ought to find some enjoyment in your day. You can borrow my skato anytime I'm not using it. I wouldn't charge you more than a penny an hour."

Which was kind of Joe, especially since he loved his skato, but Hannah knew that math itself was her one pure enjoyment. With sharpened focus and speed, egged on by Mr. Cole's enthusiasm, she redoubled her efforts. She constructed bases, built areas, balanced equations, and memorized the laws of right angles and the hypotenuse. The answer was there, its question a lock to be picked and pried. Natural, integer, rational, real. The answer was always waiting and perfect and standing alone.

In some ways, Hannah thought, studying was like milking. If you weren't concentrating on the task in hand, the twitch of a cow tail or buzz of a fly or jump of a cat could shock and tip you smack off your stool.

Don't tip, she scolded herself, and then she tapped under her desk eight times, for luck, and then another eight, and then another, and another, until she had to jump up from her desk with her hands squeezed together to make herself stop.

32

A GLASS WISH

"I LOST IT IN THE war," said Mr. Cole abruptly on the afternoon of their final lesson.

Hannah looked up from her paper. "Lost what?"

"My eye," said Mr. Cole. "Grazed by a German Maxim MG. It fires six hundred rounds of bullets per minute, but it only took one bullet to cancel my vision."

She put down her pencil. Mr. Cole had never spoken of anything so personal before. He spoke of math, and sometimes of his other passion, coffee—Mr. Cole's favorite coffee was a roasted bean from the Yakima Valley in Washington, almost impossible to get hold of. But he never spoke of the Great War.

"Would you like to see it?" he asked. On her surprised look, he offered, "I'll hold my hand over the socket, so as not to scare you. Because," he explained, "it's my superstition that if a scholarship candidate holds my eye and makes a wish, it might come true. Well, frankly," he added, now looking slightly embarrassed, "I've never taught a scholarship candidate."

Hannah nodded agreement. "I can see how you might consider your glass eye to be a lucky charm, sir," she said. "Like my thirty-two."

Mr. Cole looked pleased to hear it. He set down his chalk, turned his back, and in the next moment had pivoted around to face her again. He dropped the eye into Hannah's open palm as his other hand patched tight over his eyeless socket.

Hannah cupped Mr. Cole's eye. Warm and marbled blueish-green, it was heavier than she would have imagined. She stared hard into the oblong eye that had watched her so unflinchingly all these weeks. An eye that had checked her homework and looked for her mistakes and remembered to find the places to praise her, too.

It might be an object through which to see the future. Or, yes, even something to make a wish on.

"You must have been in shocking pain, sir," she said. "A horrible thing, to lose an eye."

"I would have given more," Mr. Cole answered quickly. "It's not much to sacrifice, one eye, if it brings hope that the futures of our children are safe from war. I hope never to bear witness to another."

Hannah placed the eyeball in Mr. Cole's palm and he turned away. When he faced her again, he was his regular, two-eyed self. "Good luck tomorrow, Hannah," said Mr. Cole. "It's been difficult for you, these past few weeks. But whatever the result, it is always important to test your mettle."

The shock of his words made her flinch. Why, he believes that I will fail, she realized in a pulse of fresh unease. "Mr. Cole, if I don't get that scholarship, am I finished forever?" she blurted. "It happened to my friend Beverly. She never got a second chance. Who's to say where I go next?"

It seemed to her that Mr. Cole's answer came rushed, as if he had given thought to the matter. "Well now, Hannah, second chances are not impossible," he said. "There are other schools and other scholarships, if you know how and where to look. Just last week, I read of plans to initiate a Marie Curie Fellowship, that will be particularly encouraging of young female scientists and mathematicians."

Hannah bit her lip. "Before he got sick, my granddad McNaughton knew of a school up in Boston. Perhaps I could look into that." Speaking Granddad's name set an immediate lump in her throat, and she twisted her fingers together, trying to resist the urge to tap.

Then she could not help herself and she tapped the sides of her chair.

Mr. Cole did not reprimand her. "Boston, exactly. Follow up on your tips and leads, as the newsmen say. Now." The gaze of Mr. Cole's sighted and glass eye bore into her. "Did you make a wish?"

Hannah nodded yes, although she had forgotten.

33

AN OTTLEY FRIEND

"**I** HAVE ONE FINAL announcement," said Miss Jordan toward the end of that afternoon's school assembly.

Soft grumbling and squeaks of shoes on the bare floor sounded in impatient protest. It was the last hour before Ottley Friends let out for the holiday break, and the assembly had been interminable, with assorted recitations, hymns, and concertos.

Plenty of style, thought Hannah, but with little of the intimacy of a Miss Cascade production.

Miss Jordan squinted from her podium and spied Hannah in a shadowy corner of the theater. Dread sent a twinge down her spine. *Don't,* her mind whispered fervently. *Don't point me out.*

Unfortunately, Miss Jordan was no mind reader. "Hannah Bennett, will you stand up a moment, please?"

Reluctant, mortified, Hannah rose to her feet while the speculating eyes of the other girls met hers as they turned to stare. Whatever this was about, she wished she had been warned! Personal appearance had not been first in her thoughts these past weeks. After two months' growth, her bobbed hair exactly resembled the haystack Roy had called it. Besides which, she was wearing her same wrinkled middy from yesterday. She probably looked as if she had been receiving fashion tips straight from Mr. Cole.

Beaming and oblivious, Miss Jordan lifted her voice. "Everyone knows that Hannah Bennett has been our guest here at Ottley Friends as she prepares for the very difficult

Wexler scholarship exam that is taking place tomorrow. Mr. Cole has declared that Hannah's achievement in mathematics is equal to a college student's. I, too, can vouch that her progress in other subjects has won my confidence." Miss Jordan's smile raised Hannah's own hopes. "Girls, join me in wishing Hannah good luck tomorrow."

"Good luck tomorrow, Hannah," sang the uninspired chorus. Yet some of the girls' gazes lingered, even after Hannah mumbled her thanks and ducked deep into her seat. Well, college-level mathematics was no small potatoes, as Joe would say, thought Hannah with some pride. More importantly, Miss Jordan spoke with real faith in her abilities. Perhaps the scholarship was within her reach, after all.

After the Ottley Friend's alma mater was sung and the assembly dismissed for the year, Hannah darted from the theater to avoid the gaggles of socializing and holiday plans. Halfway down the corridor, a voice stopped her.

"Hannah! Wait a minute!"

She turned.

Lillian Shay's plump cheeks were pink as she hurried to catch up. "I don't know when you're going back to . . . um . . . your country home," she started, her soft hands twisting the straps of her beaded purse, which was the Ottley fashion fad of the moment. "But some of us girls are gathering at my house tomorrow evening. It's my family's annual Christmas tree-trimming party. I'd be keen for you to come, too. That is, if you're not tired out from test taking."

Before Hannah could answer, Lillian reached into her purse and pulled from it a small green envelope. On it, the name *Miss Hannah Bennett* was neatly scripted in gold ink. As if Hannah, too, were one of Lillian's friends. For a moment, a sparkle of excitement lit inside her. She'd never been to a tree-trimming party—what fun! What a thing to tell the girls back home!

Then reason caught the better of her.

"I appreciate your charity, Lillian, but I'm

afraid I must decline," she said. "You've spelled my name wrong besides. It's Miss Tippity-tap to you girls, isn't it?"

The pink in Lillian's cheeks deepened. "I'm not offering charity. And I didn't mean to tease about your funny tapping habits, queer as they are. At least, I didn't mean for you to overhear. Oh, Hannah, do you truly think I don't know how perfectly hateful it is to wear an affliction on the outside?" she exclaimed in a burst of feeling. "Gosh, I'm forever being teased about my weight—no matter how much I'd love to be slim, it's an impossible task. Everyone's terribly hard on me for it. No one seems to understand that it's not for lack of work or will." Lillian's face was puckered with sincerity. "Hannah, if it's not too late, I'd like to make amends."

She extended her hand that held the envelope. Hannah's gold-scripted name glinted temptingly. "Please. Would you consider it?"

With careful fingers, Hannah reached out and took the invitation. Then she slipped it deep into her pocket. She swallowed; her throat had become dry with unexpected and overwhelming shyness. "Thank you, Lillian," she said. "I'm not leaving for Chadds Ford until Monday. Of course I'll consider it. And," she added honestly, "I think it's awfully nice of you to consider me, too."

34

11

O N THE MORNING of the eighteenth, Mrs. Sweet appeared in the kitchen, all dressed up with a fresh metallic rinse in her coppery-brown hair and crimson paint on her pointed fingernails.

"A valet from the garage is bringing around the Packard," she bellowed. "We'll all drive to Thomas Jefferson High School together. It's an important day to be spot on the dot! Hurry and finish your breakfasts. I'll be waiting outside."

Joe rolled his eyes, but did not say anything

as he and Hannah cleared their dishes, collected their coats, and joined Mrs. Sweet outside on the front stoop.

"I've got terrible butterflies," whispered Hannah low enough so that Mrs. Sweet, plucking dry leaves from her window box, did not hear her.

"Naw, it's a banner day for test taking," Joe answered cheerfully as he tugged his cap lower on his head. He inhaled and pounded his chest. "The air's so clean, it even smells like pencil shavings. And there's the car!" he announced as it swung rakishly around the curb.

Hannah had to suppress a smile when she noticed that Mrs. Sweet's precious automobile was being driven around by none other than Joe's friend Francis, who took Mrs. Sweet's ten-cent tip with a wink in Joe's direction, before touching his cap and dashing off.

"It's a super job, I hear. Tips galore," Joe whispered. "But if Sweet saw Fran steer a skato, she'd never let him inside fifty feet of her precious Packard." Joe smirked as he and Hannah climbed into the backseat.

"Try not to muss the leather," warned Mrs. Sweet. "Hands on your laps."

"Truth be told, I never rode in this boat before today," said Joe.

"Me, either," Hannah whispered back.

Mrs. Sweet was a careful driver, and her automobile was so padded and upholstered that the city streets and sounds reeled past like a silent movie or a dream. Hannah stared out at the landmark and lesser buildings that she had come to recognize. She bet that she could find her way through most of Philadelphia. The thought gave her quiet pleasure.

Suddenly, Mrs. Sweet's face appeared slantways in the rearview mirror.

"Whatever happens, children," she said, "it was I who spoke up for you both. I was your first sponsor. Everyone is aware of my charitable causes. It's been rumored that the mayor might appoint me Special Educational

Advisor to the City. And I'm not even a lawyer or a man. But my good works will not go unnoticed!"

"My sister, Sally, was my first real sponsor," mumbled Joe.

"Granddad McNaughton was my first real sponsor," Hannah answered. They shared a private smile as the car rolled up to Thomas Jefferson High School's brick walls and slate painted doors.

"Aw, but nobody's standing outside to see our Hollywood entrance!" Joe lamented as they climbed out.

"It's been my experience that most schools have too many children lurking around for my auto to be safe," said Mrs. Sweet. "Therefore, I'm off. Good luck, both of you. The school has arranged for a bus to take you home at the end of the day."

They both waved good-bye as Mrs. Sweet and her Packard drove off.

"By this time next year, ole Sweet won't

remember our names," said Joe. "Suppose she's a good egg, anyhow. She sees a problem and works to fix it."

"Guess that's better than most people. Well, Joe, if nothing else goes right today," said Hannah, "it was a beautiful ride."

"Don't be such a wet blanket. You gotta pass this thing, Hannah. You can't leave me stuck at 5 Delancey all by myself till June! Everything'll go swell," Joe assured.

He was wrong, though.

Problems began to shake loose and rattle Hannah right from the registration table, crowded with students of all ages. Half as many scholarships, Hannah recalled. No, it wasn't fair. Not when she looked at all of these serious, hopeful faces. It wasn't right to give out a taste of learning, as Joe said. A taste was just enough to know the strength of your appetite.

"Bennett, Bennett. Yes, here you are," said the registration proctor, a balding man squeezed too tight into a loud checkerboard suit. He crossed off

Hannah's name with his fountain pen and handed her a placard marked with the number 11.

Hannah stared at the two dark lines, straight and hard as prison bars.

"Eleven?" She took the placard and blinked. It couldn't be.

"Eee-lev-en." The proctor drew out the sound as if he were an auctioneer.

Eleven! It was the worst numbers luck she had ever faced. Not in her wildest imagination had Hannah figured that numbers would fail her.

Not today of all days.

"I'm sorry, sir," Hannah said. She held the placard from its strings so that it would not touch her. "I can't quite manage this number. I'll have to be another number."

"You can't be another number because you are Bennett, Eleven," countered the proctor. "Right after Barrington, Ten. Right before Boote, Twelve."

"Please, let me be ten or twelve," she volunteered.

"That is not the way it works, miss."

"C'mon, will ya!" The boy standing behind her butted Hannah's heel with the toe of his shoe.

"See, because a prime number can't be reduced," Hannah argued. "It's divisible only by one and itself. Eleven is an odd, upsetting sort of number for me, sir. Though perhaps somebody else might not mind it?" She did not expect the proctor to soften his position. Not with law of the alphabet on his side.

"Go on, Bennett, Eleven." The proctor pointed a finger on her.

"C'mon, Hannah." Suddenly Joe appeared next to her. He grabbed her hand and pulled her away. She could not believe her eyes.

Joe was wearing a placard marked with the number 32.

"Thirty-two! I'll trade you," she exclaimed. "Quick, before anyone sees!"

"I would, but we'd be found out in a minute, because we're alphabetized. Christmas, Hannah, you could turn all the milk in Philadelphia sour with that face."

"You don't understand! Thirty-two is *my number*. My magic number." She reached out and tapped the corners of Joe's placard. She tapped again. Then she couldn't stop.

Joe caught her fingers and held them. "There's no such thing as a magic number, Hannah. Fact is, there's no such thing as a number! You can't get bit or punched or shot or scratched by eleven, 'cause eleven is not even really here! So cut it out. Thirty-two, thirty-three, thirty-four—it doesn't make a jot of difference." He released her fingers, his face softening. "C'mon. Keep your head up. I'm only one classroom down from you. Remember, it's you against me, right?"

Hannah was speechless. She wanted to touch thirty-two again and to have some of its numbers luck rub off on her. Her fingers tapped a scrambled minuet along the sides of her legs. Her mind seemed to be made of soup, and she felt the support in her legs begin to crumble.

"Eighteen days was too few," she said.

"Stop that talk." Joe snapped his fingers in her face. "I've got a bright idea. When all this is over, don't take the bus. It's hardly two miles to Rittenhouse Park. It's cold, but it's clear. Tree weather. You just hafta get to the end of the test. Think of Baby Face! Even when he knew his gig was up, he kept right on driving. Drove himself all the way into that ditch, and all on his own will. Right?"

"Sure." Hannah frowned. Was taking this exam as bad as driving into a ditch?

A loud crowd of boys moved past them. Joe turned.

"I know that fella. Hey, there, sport! You, in the yellow shirt!" And Joe was gone, whistling, as he ran down the hall to catch up. Ready for anything.

Hannah was left alone with eleven. Her mind worked to sweeten it.

Her great-great-great-great grandfather Bennett had distinguished himself in the Battle of Brandywine with the 11th Pennsylvania Regiment.

Backward, eleven spelled *nevele*. That was pretty, although it meant nothing.

Another proctor, a woman with springy hair and plunking footstep, appeared in the crowded hall. She clapped her hands and asked that Numbers One through Twenty follow her. On a wave of other students, Hannah allowed herself to be swept along, as the woman led them to a large plain classroom at the end of the hall.

I could have been Number One, she thought. Or Twenty-one. Or any other number. Easily.

She slumped to her assigned desk. Desk Eleven. She blocked off the noises of the other students as they scuffled to their seats, or sharpened pencils at the sharpener, or loitered by the room's one sun-flooded window that gave a view of playing fields and bright blue sky. Everyone seemed a bit nervous, or lost, or out of place.

At the front of the room, the springy-haired proctor explained the rules, and then she passed out brand-new Blue Jay notebooks, one for each student. Hannah rolled her pencil in her hands, back and forth, in four sequences of eight. She tapped the corners of the book's mottled black-and-white pasteboard cover. Then she flipped through its endless blank, blue-lined pages, closed it, and tapped thirty-two again.

The morning passed in a fog of squeaking pencils and smothered coughing. Immediately, Hannah sensed that her reading would drag her down. Other students' workbook pages turned too quickly. She would not be able to keep up with them.

Worse, she could not make eleven leave. Her brain was plunging off into odd directions no matter how she tried to make it drop anchor. Pascal's Triangle could be computed in powers of eleven. 11, 121, 1331 . . .

Giving into the impulse, she tapped the corners of her placard. Eight, eight, eight, eight. Eight, eight, eight, eight. Eight, eight, eight, eight. Eight, eight, eight, eight.

Time was slipping away.

The slithery sounds of essay-writing filled her ears while she struggled through the multiple-choice section. Occasionally she cast sidelong looks at her fellow test takers. All of these girls and boys had spent the past few months living in variations of luck and upheaval, and all of them knew it would come to this day, and some of them even knew they would fail.

The pale-lashed boy sitting next to her fidgeted in his chair. Barrington, she recalled. Number Ten. The number Hannah might have been if Barrington had not existed.

At the front of the room, the proctor clanked a small cowbell. "Fifteen-minute break," she said. "Close your books. Apples and rolls are being served in the registration hall. We will resume with more reading comprehension, and then math."

Hannah shut her book and sat in her chair through the break. She bet by now Joe had made half a dozen friends.

"Psst. Hey, girl," Barrington said when he returned to his chair. "You, Bennett. Cut it out with that clicking on your card. It's distracting."

"I'll trade you my eleven for your ten," Hannah offered.

"No chance. Ten's lucky."

Hannah's stomach lurched. Even Barrington knew.

The bell rang, and the test resumed. In the next room, Hannah sensed that Joe was moving deftly through this exam, easy as fish stew. Elway, Number 32, and the Voice of Ulysses besides. He would pass this exam and the next, and the next, and on and on. Reciting, filling in the blanks, inching himself smoothly forward. He was smart and he was ready.

But she was not quite ready. She would not get this scholarship.

Not this time, but maybe next time.

The thought surprised her. Next time, yes. She would try again, and she would find her second chance. That's what Mr. Cole had been

telling her. Next year, when she knew more things. When she could read better. When she could manage her tapping easier.

If a taste was just enough to know the strength of your appetite, perhaps that was not such a bad thing, after all.

At the final clank of the bell, Hannah passed up her notebook. She apologized to Barrington for her disruptions.

He nodded, his pale eyes flickering cautiously. "Think ya did all right?"

"Better than I expected," she answered, "but I didn't pass."

"Sorry." Barrington tried to blank his face over his obvious relief.

Outside the classroom, she saw Joe, his shoulder to the wall, thick in a conversation with a group of boys. She did not want to interrupt, but she was too impatient to wait for him. She would start and he could catch up later.

Hannah buttoned her coat, pulled her beret over her ears, and pocketed a roll from the basket

at the registration table. Then she stepped through Thomas Jefferson's doors and into an ordinary beautiful winter afternoon. Piercing blue sky and needle thin air. It was almost three o'clock, and it would grow dark soon, but now there was some light and time.

Her feet carried her swiftly to Rittenhouse Park. Along the way, she counted off all of the beautiful objects in the city. The iron gates, the fire hydrants, the cars and carts and horses and street signs and storefront awnings. The city ticked and clacked and hummed and made a different pattern every day. It was always changing, there was no fixed and final answer, and, actually, she had come to appreciate it, because she was the same way.

I'll find the right doors and I'll push them as hard as I can, she thought. Math is everywhere, and it has always belonged to me if I wanted it. And now I know that I do, more than anything. I'll go anywhere for it.

At the gate's entrance, Hannah kicked off her

shoes and rolled her socks into a ball. Her bare feet sang with cold as she walked across the grass to her willow tree. She tested a hand to its base and caught hold of one branch. Pulled herself up and caught another.

Up and up.

Climbing a tree was the silliest thing in the world. It didn't really get a person to anywhere in particular, and once up, you were immediately presented with the puzzle of how to get down.

That hardly mattered, though. What did matter was that she had found a perfect place to enjoy a perfect hour. She pressed her nose against the bark, inhaling the scent of the tree and the faint woods of where it came from. Then she swung her legs free, back and forth, delighting in the fresh air on her skin and the wide-open view of the city, as she waited for Joe to join her.

AUTHOR'S NOTE

For their tremendous assistance with the particular details of this story, I thank my editor, Donna Bray, as well as Brian Carey, Allison Heiny, Erich Mauff, Monica Mayper, Adele Sands, James Sands, Bill Stedman, Thorin Tritter, Kathy Wandersee, and Robert Watson. These books also were especially useful: *Since Yesterday: The 1930s in America*, by Frederick Lewis Allen; *Philadelphia Boyhood: Growing Up in the 1930s*, by Paul Hogan; *An Architectural Guidebook to Philadelphia*, by Francis Morrone with James Iska; and *Hard Times, An Oral History of the Great Depression*, by Studs Terkel. Additional guidance was provided by the following Web links: "American Life Histories: Manuscripts from the Federal Writers' Project" (http://memory.loc.gov/ammem/wpaintro/wpahome.html), "The Hollywood Thirties: The Daring Films of 1930–1934" (www/geocities.com/Hollywood/Lot/4344/stage7.html), "The Original Old Time Radio" (www.old-time.com), and "The Chadds Ford Historical Society" (www.voicenet.com/~cfhs).